NORTH
OF
INFINITY
II

NORTH
OF
INFINITY
II

Edited by Mark Leslie

mosaic press

Library and Archives Canada Cataloguing in Publication

North of infinity II / edited by Mark Leslie.

ISBN 0-88962-864-5

1. Science fiction, Canadian (English). 2. Short stories, Canadian (English). 3. Canadian fiction (English)--21st century. I. Leslie, Mark, 1969-

PS8323.S3N655 2006   C813'.6   C2006-902578-9

Published by Mosaic Press, offices and warehouse at 1252 Speers Rd., units 1 & 2, Oakville, On L6L 5N9, Canada and Mosaic Press, PMB 145, 4500 Witmer Industrial Estates, Niagara Falls, NY, 14305-1386, U.S.A.
info@mosaic-press.com

Copyright © Mark Leslie Lefebvre and the Authors, 2006
Printed and Bound in Canada
ISBN 0-88962-864-5

Published by Mosaic Press
Designed by Samuel Tharmaratnam

Mosaic Press in Canada:
1252 Speers Road, Units 1 & 2,
Oakville, Ontario
L6L 5N9
Phone/Fax: 905-825-2130
info@mosaic-press.com
http://www.mosaic-press.com

Mosaic Press in U.S.A.:
4500 Witmer Industrial Estates
PMB 145, Niagara Falls, NY
14305-1386
Phone/Fax: 1-800-387-8992
info@mosaic-press.com
http://www.mosaic-press.com

www.mosaic-press.com

To Don Hutchison:
for continually raising the bar

&

To Alexander Leslie:
may you never lose your sense of wonder

Mark Leslie

About the Editor

Since 1999 a good portion of Mark Leslie's writing and editing efforts have been conducted during the three hours per day he spends commuting via GO transit between his home in Hamilton and his day job within the IT Supply Chain team at Indigo Books & Music Inc.

In the early 1990's Mark was assistant editor of *North-Words* magazine and co-editor of *Northern Fusion* magazine. Although writing is his first passion, he compares his return to editing and reading unsolicited submissions to the joy and thrill of finding presents under the tree on Christmas morning. 'Sometimes, the wait can be unbearable, but the treasures that can be reaped are worth every moment.'

Mark's fiction has appeared in such anthologies as *Stardust* and *Bluffs*. His writing has been short-listed for an Aurora Award and he has received honorable mention in The Year's Best Fantasy & Horror. In 2004 Mark released a collection of his previously published horror fiction and dark poetry in a book from Stark Publishing entitled *One Hand Screaming*. He has recently completed Morning Son, a contemporary fiction and is hard at work at a science fiction thriller and a humorous mystery novel.

In January 2006, Mark began unrolling the serial thriller 'I, Death' online in blog format at http://this-mortal-coil.blogspot.com. A novella based on 'I, Death' which will include the sequel to the world-renowned online thriller as well as related erotic horror tales is forthcoming from Mosaic Press.

Mark lives in Hamilton, Ontario, with his wife, their son and a little dwarf rabbit named Mister Bunny. Online he can be found at www.markleslie.ca and in the blogosphere at http://markleslie.blogspot.com.

Table of Contents

Preface

State of Disorder
     by Douglas Smith   Page 1

Pas de deux
     by Stephen Graham King   Page 18

The Identity Factory
     by Andrew Weiner   Page 28

Shadows
     by Karen Danylak   Page 41

I Found Love on Channel 3
     by Bruce Golden   Page 51

Metal Fatigue
     by Nancy Kilpatrick   Page 60

Son of Sun
     by A. M. Matte   Page 67

Lumps
     by Robert H. Beer   Page 72

Confessions of Me: Betrayer of Humanity
     by Zohar A. Goodman   Page 81

Forever
     by Robert J. Sawyer   Page 90

(continued over)

The Sum of Their Parts
    by Stephanie Bedwell-Grime   Page 100

Waltrer's Brain
    by Kimberly Foottit   Page 112

Preface

A funny thing happened on the way to infinity.

North of Infinity was published by Mosaic Press in 1998. It was to be followed in late 1999 by North of Infinity II as the world faced a new century and new millennium. Its theme was trepidation felt during times of great change or crossroads.

Naturally fitting, of course.

The year 2000 came, and there was no great apocalyptic change, nor did the Y2K bug get the better of us.

North of Infinity II didn't surface either.

After a period of time I like to think of as a few minutes south of yesterday, I was transformed from contributor to series editor. And the anthology that was concerned with exploring "change" underwent a change of its own.

Again, quite fitting.

At about the same time I was taking over this series my personal life was undergoing a significant change. I became a father. It's an experience that has helped me grow in ways that defy description, but it also helped me in rounding out the selection for this anthology. Ultimately, I wanted to find stories that not only adhered to the theme, but filled me with the same sense of wonder I remember feeling when first reading a story by Ray Bradbury or Lester del Rey; the sense of wonder I catch a glimpse of in my son's eyes as he discovers new things about the world around him. It's what I'm hoping can be captured with each new edition of this series.

As the French say, "Plus ca change, plus c'est la meme chose" (the more things change, the more they stay the same). How very fitting, then, that the theme for this collection is about crossroads, about change, about turning points. It's the perfect theme to allow a series to undergo its own editorial change, and yet continue in a direction it was already headed. That indefinable yet wondrous place that rests just north of infinity.

The stories you are about to read concern themselves with change, or crossroads. Science fiction is often a playground for ideas of "what if?" examining the effect of technological, societal or personal change. This collection is no exception. All of the tales examine either a change directly affecting a single character or the result of a technological or societal change. Sure, it's a pretty wide-open, seemingly all-inclusive theme. But the tales our authors tell are worthy of telling and being showcased together.

On the pages that follow you will find narratives about a man able to send messages to himself in the past and alter his own destiny, a future society devoid of the female gender, a society in which purchasing a new personality/identity is the norm, and the first global change that wiped out an entire species on our planet. You'll find those tales as well as other great speculative stories that concern themselves with change and inspire a sense of wonder. Some stories are by recognizable science fiction names whose reprinted tales are worth bringing back into print, and others are by authors whose work you might not have seen before, but whose stories are certainly worth discovering. A continued goal of this anthology series is to offer quality stories, whether they are from established names or from up and coming writers whose efforts you might be enjoying for the first time. I think North of Infinity 2 does that nicely.

So, with your eyes of childhood and sense of wonder firmly in place, I invite you to turn and face the strange. Enjoy.

Mark Leslie
April 2006

State of Disorder

by Douglas Smith

Douglas Smith is a Toronto-based writer whose stories have appeared in over sixty professional magazines and anthologies in twenty-four countries and twenty languages around the world. In Canada, his work has appeared in the literary magazine, *Prairie Fire*, and the speculative fiction magazines, *On Spec* and Solaris, as well as the TESSERACTS, SKY SONGS, and WONDER ZONE anthology series. Outside of Canada, his work has appeared in *The Third Alternative, InterZone, The Year's Best New Horror, Amazing Stories, Cicada*, and anthologies from Penguin, DAW, and other publishers. In 2001, Doug was a finalist for the international John W. Campbell Award for best new writer. His stories have twice won the Aurora Award, Canada's top award for speculative short fiction. Doug is currently working on his first novel. His web site is www.smithwriter. com and he may be contacted at doug@smithwriter.com.

"State of Disorder" originally appeared in Amazing Stories #595

And thus the whirligig of time brings in his revenges.
- Shakespeare, *Twelfth Night*

Tick.

In the banquet hall of a sprawling castle of a house, the woman looks up, startled. The dishes of the night's dinner still litter the long table before her. At the evening's outset, the table had been so clean, its settings so precise. She tries to recall each step in its journey from order to chaos but fails.

Tick.

She jumps again at the sound. A man's wristwatch lies at the table's far end. He has left it, forgotten or unwanted. Or for another reason. The watch is old with a broken strap; the woman young with a broken heart. The watch lies face down, but she knows it is the old-fashioned kind with hands. A date will show in a little window. A date from a time long ago. Two lives ago. It will be today's date. She wonders how she knows that.

Tick.

Rising, she moves toward the watch...

#

"My God, James. Look at this place," Caroline exclaimed.

James Mackaby put down the book he was reading to their young son, David, and looked out the window of their limousine. Their driver was negotiating a street filled with refuse and the abandoned corpses of burnt-out cars. Under a late afternoon sun, men in ragged clothing slept or sprawled on steps before low-rise apartments. The nearest group of men shouted something at the car as they passed around a bottle.

The limousine pulled up to the curb in front of a dirty-gray, three-storied building. Crumbling steps led to a door with a crisscross of planks covering its broken glass. Mackaby surveyed the scene and looked back to his wife. "Looks like Dr. Harnish has fallen lower than I thought."

"Are you sure it's wise to go?" Caroline asked. "He was very uncivil to you when the University dismissed him."

Mackaby felt uneasy at the memory. But for her sake, he forced a smile. "He was treating everyone that way by then."

"Still..."

"And he's asking for my help now. Besides, I can't cancel a dinner this late, though I know better ways to spend an evening." He grinned and she smiled, rubbing her foot against his. He gave David a hug. "Bye-bye, my big man. Be good."

David hugged him back. "Can we read my story later, Daddy?"

"Daddy won't be back until past bedtime, dear. We'll read it tomorrow." He pulled Caroline to him in a long kiss, then stepped from the car into cool fall air, her perfume swirling in his head. He spoke to their driver. "Pick me up at ten o'clock sharp. Apartment 202. If you need to, call me on my cell."

The driver nodded.

Caroline leaned out the back window. "Wait. I have your watch. They fixed it but won't have a strap till next week." She took a man's wristwatch from her purse. Gold hands, black face, broken leather strap. The inscription on the back read, "To James, forever your Caroline."

Caroline stared at the building. "James, do you..."

Mackaby kissed her again. "I'll see you before midnight." He put the watch in his pocket and climbed the steps. At the door he stopped to wave to them, but the big Lincoln was already gone. He lowered his hand, his feeling of unease returning.

#

Tick.

The sound no longer startles her. She walks the length of the table to stand beside where the watch lies.

#

The door to the building squealed open with rusty protests at his tugging. Mackaby stepped into a small vestibule, catching his breath on the stink of urine and sweat. A filthy blanket lay on the floor. Mackaby scanned a row of room buttons, half of which showed neither names nor numbers. Finding one for 210, he counted back to what he hoped was 202. Response was immediate.

"Is that you, Mackaby?"

"Yes, Doctor." He wondered if Harnish had been watching.

A harsh buzz sounded, and the inner door admitted Mackaby to a lobby of stained wallpaper and couches sprouting foam rubber and springs. The elevator was out of order, so he climbed sagging steps to a musty second-floor hall lit by random dim bulbs. He walked along, peering at room numbers. A door opened as he passed but closed quickly when he turned.

Reaching room 202, he knocked. The door opened, and Dr. Roderick Harnish stood before him. Mackaby tried to hide the shock he felt. It had been two years since they had last met. Two years can be a long time, Mackaby realized.

A faded blue robe hung on Harnish's stooped and shrunken frame. Prematurely white hair thrown straight back fell to rounded shoulders. Under his robe he wore a shirt, once white, with a tie knotted off-center at his neck. Gray slacks with a cuff in need of stitching and dirty brown slippers completed his attire. He thrust out a thin hand that Mackaby fumbled to grip. "Dr. Mackaby! So good of you to come." The older man's voice held a strength that belied his frail aspect. And the eyes in that sallow face burnt as brightly as Mackaby had remembered.

Harnish ushered him into a small living room. A kitchen stood to the right. To the left, a hall led to a bathroom and the closed door of another room. Taking Mackaby's coat, Harnish stroked the material. "A quality garment. How wonderful that you can afford the finer things, eh? For me, well, I must make do with less." He hung the coat in an empty closet. "Please, please, come in and sit. We shall have a drink before dinner."

A few steps brought Mackaby to the center of the small room's bare floor. The reek of onions now assailed him. He attempted a smile. "Dinner smells wonderful, Doctor."

Harnish motioned him to one of two threadbare armchairs. A small table stood between them, a lamp with a torn shade perched near one corner and a book beside it. "Sit, sit. Ah, yes. Well, dinner will be a simpler fare than that to which you are no doubt accustomed. However, I have learned to hide the quality of the meat with some simple sauces." Harnish chuckled as if this preview of their meal would please his guest. "Now, perhaps a scotch, a sherry? I still allow myself those luxuries."

"A sherry, please." Settling into a chair that groaned in protest, Mackaby surveyed the room. Water stains and peeling paint marked walls unadorned by art or decoration. He peeked at the book that lay on the table. Short stories by Poe, opened to *The Cask of Amontillado*.

From a scratched wooden cabinet, Harnish removed a near-empty bottle and two glasses. He walked to the only other piece of furniture in the room, a dining table set for two, and poured the sherry. Handing Mackaby a glass, he settled into the chair beside him, smiling at his guest. "So."

Mackaby felt awkward. "Uh, yes. So. So..."

Harnish threw his head back, laughing. "No need for small talk, sir. Neither of us was ever good at it." Leaning forward, he tapped Mackaby's knee with a bony finger. "I will tell you what prompted my invitation that you were so gracious to accept."

Mackaby tasted his sherry. Dry but of poor quality. "I understood that you wish reinstatement to the faculty and hope that I will plead your case, due to my position on the Board."

Harnish smiled. "I intend for you to play a role in my return to grace, yes." The smile left his face as he spoke. "Do you recall the Amsterdam Conference?"

Mackaby frowned. "I didn't attend. It was, what, five years ago?" Mackaby felt his sense of disquiet return.

"Five years," Harnish said, glancing to where a picture of a woman stood on a small television. Mackaby recalled that Harnish had been married. She had left him after his dismissal. Harnish continued. "You and I were approaching our zeniths. On different courses in related fields but both destined, it seemed, to become part of scientific history." He took a sip. "History. An appropriate topic, considering that conference."

"I don't follow you, Doctor," Mackaby said, letting a touch of the irritation he was feeling creep into his voice.

"Indulge me," Harnish said with a smile. "Do you remember the paper I tabled at that conference?"

Mackaby searched his memory. "I believe that it dealt with Hawking's concept of the thermodynamic arrow of time, the time direction in which disorder or entropy increases."

Harnish nodded. "Hawking argued that entropy also dictates our psychological arrow of time, our sense of temporal direction. We remember events in the order in which entropy increases, because we must. This makes the second law of thermodynamics irrelevant.

Disorder increases with time because we measure time in the direction of increasing disorder."

Mackaby relaxed a bit, his unease now lost in his intellect. "Yes, I remember. You argued that if one could reverse the state of disorder in a closed system, that is, decrease the entropy, then the system would move backwards on the time continuum."

"Backwards on the human perception of the time line, yes."

"As I remember, that part of your work was well accepted."

Harnish dismissed this with a wave of his hand. "That was trivial. Obvious. Do you recall the real crux of my paper?"

Knowing where this was leading, Mackaby sighed. "You proposed a closed system in which you could reverse entropy, via antimatter bombardment, I believe. I don't recall the details."

Harnish stared at him unblinking for several breaths. "You don't recall the details," he repeated. "Well, Amsterdam was a long time ago. And as you point out, you did not attend, thus missing the impact your work here had on my own." The smile that twitched at his lips did not reach his eyes.

Mackaby's mouth felt dry. He took a drink. "My work at the time dealt with an obscure offshoot of research into black holes. True, it dealt with entropic boundary issues but --"

"Your research illuminated a flaw in my theory, Mackaby. Boundary definition. Thelbrond of MIT picked up on it in his paper, presented after my own. I proved that my method would reduce the entropy of all matter contained within my shielded system. However, Thelbrond showed that the entropy of the shielding wall containing this matter would increase, offsetting this reduction." His lips quivered. "*Total* entropy within my system would increase, not decrease."

Mackaby said nothing, unable to look away from Harnish's gaze. His hand felt hot and sticky on the sherry glass.

"Thelbrond destroyed my career. Using your work, Mackaby. That, too, is now part of *history*." Harnish spoke as a scientist noting an experimental result, merely reporting an entry in a journal. If the man felt anything, his face did not betray it.

Still, Mackaby felt a chill. "Doctor, I did not realize that Thelbrond had leveraged my early research against you."

Harnish preempted him with an upheld hand. "I do not accuse but simply state the facts. After Amsterdam, I faced ridicule at subsequent symposiums and within the faculty. Eventually, I was refused funding." Rising, he walked to the small window. Coarse burlap, strung from uneven rods above, posed as curtains. He stared at the street below. An uneasy silence, as ugly as the window coverings, hung between them. Mackaby was about to end the strange evening when Harnish turned back to him. "Such a lovely neighborhood. I fear I will forget it." Harnish motioned him to the table. "Please sit. I will serve."

Pondering the odd remark, Mackaby took his place, facing the kitchen. To discreetly monitor the hour, he placed his watch with the broken strap in front of him. A microwave beeped. Harnish returned with two steaming bowls. They ate in silence, the soup a thin potato cream, too salty for Mackaby's taste.

Harnish chuckled, and Mackaby looked up. A crooked smile twisted the man's lip. "Do you know, Mackaby, how I spent my remaining funds after Amsterdam?"

Mackaby shook his head. "You have published no paper since that conference. You fired your assistants --"

"They betrayed me," Harnish interrupted in a low tone. "Telling my secrets to my enemies, stealing my ideas..."

He is mad, Mackaby thought. "Yes, well, in any event, you then worked alone. No one knew how you directed your energies."

His host's smile held no warmth. "Then tonight shall bring revelation." Under his breath, almost inaudible, he added, "and much, much more." He stared hard at Mackaby, then around him, as if seeing the room for the first time, a grimace contorting his face. "Enough. It is time," he muttered. Rising, he hobbled to the narrow hall leading to the closed door of the second room.

Mackaby heard a key turn and a door open and close. Then nothing. He waited. Still nothing. His patience exhausted, he rose, intending to leave. Remembering his watch, he turned back to the table. And stopped. The timepiece was nowhere to be seen. He searched the table and floor, but in vain.

The watch was gone.

A low buzz rose above the street noise and climbed quickly to a high-pitched whining. A tingling sensation shot up his spine. Vertigo and weakness flooded him. He slumped back into his chair, knocking the table, spilling his sherry. The stain spread across the tablecloth where his watch had lain.

A noise brought his head up. Splitting diagonally, the wall beside the kitchen door pulled apart. Behind the crack appeared not a view into the tiny kitchen, but an empty whiteness. Mute with terror, Mackaby struggled again to his feet. As he stumbled to the door, the small room stretched away from him. Details thinned, edges blurred, colors faded. With a shriek, the scene shattered like a mirror struck by a hammer. Jagged shards of reality spun into a white void. He heard his son David call "Daddy," heard himself scream, felt himself falling, felt...

Nothing.

#

Tick.

She wonders idly how it can sound so loud, this little watch. Perhaps, she thinks, I only hear it in my mind. This thought does not concern her.

She reaches for the watch...

#

Mackaby wiped his mouth on a fine linen napkin as the final notes of a Vivaldi concerto wafted from the stereo. "Excellent risotto, Doctor. My compliments to your chef."

Harnish picked a thread from his dinner jacket, smiling thinly down the dining room table. "Not my chef, I'm afraid, Mackaby. Such extravagances are yet beyond me. However, I did take the liberty of hiring a caterer."

Harnish had been the perfect host, yet Mackaby still felt uncomfortable. "You shouldn't have gone to such expense, sir."

Harnish's pale lips curled into a one-cornered smile. "I assure you, such items are trifles compared to my other efforts toward this evening." He rang a small silver bell. A uniformed servant appeared through French doors behind him. The man removed the plates, disappearing again into the kitchen.

Mackaby looked over his host again. Short-cropped graying hair on a square head set on a body still ramrod straight as in his youth. "That is the second reference you've made, Doctor, to a singular aspect of this evening. Just what is the occasion?"

"Why, the anniversary of this dinner!" Harnish ignored the puzzled look Mackaby knew he wore. "Mind you, 'anniversary' is not quite correct. A true term does not exist since the event has no precedent. Or rather, as only I know of its occurrence, only I require a word to describe it." He smiled.

Mackaby felt confused. "I do not understand you, Doctor."

Harnish rose and walked to the long wall of floor-to-ceiling windows. Pulling back a lace curtain with a manicured hand, he stared down at the street. Mackaby wondered what could have caught his attention, lovely though the tree-lined boulevard and sculpture garden were.

"You do not remember our first dinner, on this very date, do you?" Harnish asked, his back still to his guest.

Mackaby felt his patience waning. "What do you mean?"

Harnish turned to look at him again. "Pity. It would be so much more satisfying if you remembered it all. I suppose I will have to make do with telling you. Once I am done, that is."

His anger building, Mackaby rose to face the smaller man. "Doctor, I accepted your invitation based on your promise to discuss my reinstatement to the faculty, which you said you could arrange due to your reputation and position. I now find --"

Harnish raised a hand to stop him. "How is your wife, dear boy? Caroline? Lovely girl, that."

Taken aback, Mackaby stammered out, "She is quite well, since you ask. She has had to take a job due to my situation --"

"And your son?"

Mackaby blinked. "We have no children. Neither of us wished to begin a family until I was certain of a steady income." He recovered his composure. "Doctor, I must insist you --"

Again Harnish cut him off with an imperious wave. "Enough. It is time. Again." Without even excusing himself, Harnish departed through the adjacent study. His steps echoed down the tiled hall leading to his private rooms.

Mackaby stood stunned by his host's rude and odd behavior. Then his anger returned and he determined to leave at once. As he crossed the dining room threshold, dizziness seized him and a piercing whistle stung his ears. Grasping at a door frame that writhed away from his hand, he pitched forward as the room began to melt, to flow. Colors and shapes swirled into each other like a nightmare soup of reality stirred by a cosmic hand. An image of Caroline, crying, whirled by in the vortex. Her tears became streaks of blood as the maelstrom pulled her image and him down into it, down toward a singularity of pure white nothingness.

\#

Tick.

She holds the watch -- and begins to shake. Emotions flow into her or out of her, she isn't sure which. Crying out, she slumps to the floor to lie sobbing, praying for them to end. They cease but only when she is numbed of resistance. Then the pictures come, and sounds, smells, touches, like waves of forgotten dreams. Of a man she loved. Of a child. Their child.

Tick.

Her hand unclenches. The watch falls to the carpet. She wonders where the man has gone, what has happened to her son.

\#

Having finished the last crumb of his cake, Mackaby put down his fork. Harnish's uniformed butler whisked his plate and cutlery away. Looking up, Mackaby was startled to see Harnish's gaze fixed on him from the end of the long table.

"Hungry, Mackaby?" His eyes seemed to hold a secret joke.

"Roderick! You're embarrassing our guest." Caroline rose from where she sat beside Harnish, smiling at Mackaby. "I'll leave you two alone. Roderick will want his after-dinner cigar, and I have never become used to them."

Mackaby watched her leave, his mind drifting to the ache in his heart like a tongue searching for a missing tooth. Feeling Harnish's eyes on him, Mackaby muttered, "Please excuse me, Doctor. I have not had such a meal in some time."

"Time. Yes. A long time. Five years since I last had the opportunity to host you." The amused expression remained.

Mackaby hesitated, not certain how to respond. "I don't recall another instance when I have been your guest."

Harnish chuckled. "Tonight is the third time we have dined on this very date. Although . . ." -- he paused, gesturing around the opulent dining hall -- ". . . the decor has improved over the first of these feasts." Mackaby stared at him. Grinning, Harnish rose. "Come into the library. Tonight all shall be made clear."

Limping even with his cane, Mackaby followed him out of the dining room. Harnish stopped at the door to the library. "Ah! My apologies. I forgot how your injury has slowed you. I would have thought it healed by now."

Mackaby grimaced, trying to hide the pain he felt. "Arthritis in the knee is the main difficulty now, Doctor."

In the large study, Harnish motioned to a high-backed leather chair. Seating himself beside Mackaby, his feet on an ottoman, the older man pulled a cigar from his jacket. "Terrible thing, that plane crash, though I suppose you count yourself lucky, surviving at all. Fortunate your wife was not with you."

Mackaby looked at a painting over the fireplace. Caroline, in a blue evening dress, sat in a velvet chair. Harnish, in a tuxedo, stood behind her. Mackaby remembered when she had been his. He had planned to ask her to marry him once he became established. Then fate had turned against him. He looked back to his host. "You know I have never married."

Harnish was studying his face intently, amusement flickering behind every twitch. "Ah, yes. Silly of me." Lighting the cigar, Harnish settled into the chair. "Now, for a story. Actually three stories, although you still remember the third, so I will not bore you with that."

"I still remember... What do you mean?"

Harnish grinned through his smoke. "Why, your life, Mackaby. Or to be precise, three lives, two of which no longer exist." He put down his cigar and from a pocket removed a man's wristwatch. Holding it, he stroked it like a beloved pet. "Imagine an event which unalterably changes the balance of your life, all that you could have become, all you might have been. You would expect such an event to be memorable, would you not?"

Mackaby felt confused. And something else. He felt the beginning of fear. Irrational. He swallowed but said nothing.

Caressing the watch, Harnish continued. "Your memories of this event could be of either joy or regret, depending on the direction it moved your destiny. You and I, Mackaby, have lived through three such events, all on the very same day, all quite different, except in the aspect of the fortunes each visited upon my future. And misfortunes on yours."

Harnish placed the watch on a table between them. Mackaby fought an urge to pull away. Through a haze of sudden nausea, he realized Harnish was talking again. "... say 'future,' like most fools, you extrapolate a continued existence from your present state to a better one, a transformation you effect by dreams and ignorance. I have dealt with my futures. This evening, I am concerned only with our pasts."

Mackaby felt dazed, his limbs weak. A loud ticking filled his head. "What are you talking about?" he whispered.

Harnish chuckled. "After Amsterdam, I invested my remaining funds in researching the role of entropy in other branches of science." He pushed the watch closer, and Mackaby struggled to pull his hand away. Grinning, Harnish continued. "My work led me to communications theory, where signal repetition introduces increasing disorder -- entropy -- in the signal."

A fire played in Harnish's eyes as the scientist supplanted the man. "I theorized a closed system in which I could generate a wave form of electromagnetic radiation displaying decreased entropy. Such a wave form would move backwards with respect to our psychological arrow of time, our perception of time flow. If I could then modulate the wave form, I would have a transmitter. I would, in short, be able to send a message back in time."

Mackaby struggled to form words as the watch's ticking swarmed in his ears. He felt he must shout to be heard, but could only whisper. "Backwards to where? Who would be listening?"

"I would, Mackaby. I would also build a receiver and wait in that squalid little apartment after Amsterdam for the Roderick Harnish of years yet to be to send a message. Can you guess the content of that message?" Retrieving the watch again, Harnish dangled it in front of Mackaby. Mackaby sat frozen, terrified he would touch the thing. His mind cried such fear was baseless, but a more primal part knew better.

"No answer? Then I shall tell you." Harnish's face became as stone. "I would direct my younger self into research to bring him accolades, not contempt. I would direct his finances to bring him wealth." Harnish leaned closer. Mackaby could smell his sour breath. "And I would provide young Roderick with knowledge to use against those who had wronged me. Those who had mocked my work, had lied to me and about me." Voice breaking, his jaw tightened. "Those who had ruined my life."

Harnish sat back, the watch swinging like Poe's pendulum blade from his fingers. "Problems arose. I found that I had but certain windows of opportunity to transmit to my earlier self. Using my own new branch of mathematics, I computed the first date when I might transmit. Can you guess that date, Mackaby?"

Mackaby knew but could not speak. Harnish reached out to lay the watch across the arm of Mackaby's chair. Cringing into the far corner of his seat, Mackaby barely dared to breathe. Apparently oblivious, Harnish rose and began pacing the room.

"Today, Mackaby, today. And since you authored my decline, I chose you to share the fruits of my labor. I followed your work and that of your contemporaries. As expected, research emerged four years later refuting your early papers after Amsterdam. Simply the progress of science -- we stand on the shoulders of those who went before. But if such results came out earlier, coincident with your own? You would look the fool, an incompetent bungler. And the scientist who published the correct results? His star would be in the ascendant. I was that person, Mackaby. I destroyed you, taking your position and reputation. And much more." He paused before the portrait of Caroline.

"What do you mean?" Mackaby whispered. "I never had a position at the University. . . ."

Returning to his chair, Harnish lit another cigar. "Having determined the transmittal date, I invited you to dinner. Early that evening, I left you and entered my machine -- my closed system -- to send my message back five years. I assumed Harnish-the-sender would vanish the moment I transmitted, since my earlier self would take actions based on my message to prevent my current present from ever occurring. In my new life, I would recall receiving but not sending my message. My current memories would not exist, since I had never lived that life. Such was my belief as I pressed the button to transmit."

Mackaby's eyes flitted between Harnish's grin and the watch that lay so close. The ticking punctuated each word of the tale.

"What happened? Nothing. I felt no change whatsoever. With a bitter heart, I stepped from my machine. And into a new world! I stood in an affluent suburban home. Feeling faint, I looked down.

My hands, arms, my very body seemed transparent, insubstantial. I was fading. As this occurred, strange thoughts, conversations, images deluged my brain -- new memories, if such a term can be used. A moment of vertigo; then I found myself seated across from you at dinner. I recalled all of my new life after young Harnish had received my message, yet I retained memories of my now-extinct prior life as well. I theorized that the closed system had protected my old memories. On leaving the machine, my old self had merged into my new self."

Harnish plucked the watch from the chair arm. For a moment, Mackaby feared Harnish would touch him with it, and his breath caught in his throat. But the older man just sat back and began speaking again, holding the watch in front of him.

"I had not expected to optimize my life with one try. Now the last five years of my new life filled my head -- a source for a second message, to fine tune my past. And yours. For I 'remembered' deciding to reenact our dinner on the 'anniversary' of when my new life truly began and when I would again have a window to transmit. We had just finished our first course. I stayed for the next, then left again to send my second message. I emerged to this." Harnish swirled his hand and the watch through the air. "Again I melded with my new self, retaining full recall of my now two prior lives. And so, we come to the third instance of this extraordinary dinner."

Mackaby beat down his terror again. "This is ludicrous. You are cruel, Doctor, to lord your success over me like this."

Harnish smiled again. "Your disbelief illustrates the sole flaw in my plan. I lose the sweetness of revenge if you remain unaware or unconvinced. So I formed a theory, now to be tested." He fingered the watch. "At our first dinner, I took this watch from you and into my closed system. It remained there through each transmission, until tonight when I retrieved it."

Mackaby fought for breath against the grip of fear on his throat. Harnish continued. "I hypothesized that if an object of yours from the original time stream was in my system when I transmitted, the object might retain a link to your soon-to-be erased past." Harnish leaned forward to dangle the watch before Mackaby's sweating face. "After all, this is all that remains of that first life you once led. All else was wiped clean by my first message. Do you believe in psychometry, Mackaby? By holding an object, a psychic can read the lives of its prior owners. What might this watch tell you?"

The older man laid the watch again on the arm of Mackaby's chair and leaned forward. "Pick it up." His tone was one of command, but Mackaby didn't move. Not from defiance, but from fear. Harnish's breath rushed out in a sudden hiss. Grabbing Mackaby's nearer hand, he shoved the watch into the open palm and pressed Mackaby's fingers over it.

Stiffening, Mackaby tried to open his fingers, to throw the watch from him. His hand would not open, but his mouth did, to free a sob that ran screaming from his heart. A thousand faces, sounds, smells, conversations stormed his mind. He felt pain; he felt joy. He wept, laughed, lusted, loved. Scene after scene beat upon his numbed soul. And he *knew*. He knew these were his lost lives. One image hovered in front of him. He felt her lips, her skin, smelled her perfume. "Caroline," he cried as she faded. They all faded -- the pictures, memories, his lives.

Harnish was talking again. Mackaby looked up at the older man hovering over him and realized he had fallen to the floor.

"Sweet excellence!" Harnish clasped his hands before him. "The missing element is delivered to me. Awareness in my victim." He knelt beside Mackaby. "Caroline was your wife," Harnish whispered. "You had a child named David. You were a giant in your field. Your patents had made you a rich man. I took all that from you, Mackaby. I took it for myself."

Feeling his nausea rise, Mackaby forced himself to his hands and knees just as he threw up on the carpet. When his retching stopped, he wiped his mouth on the sleeve of his threadbare jacket and stood. Trembling with anger and horror, tasting the foulness in his mouth, he faced his foe. But Harnish stared past Mackaby, his face like stone again.   Mackaby turned.

Caroline stood in the doorway, a hand on the door frame, eyes wide. "Roderick, I heard my name . . ." she began. Mackaby could not tell if it was a question or an accusation.

Harnish pulled himself up tall. "Caroline, I regret that Doctor Mackaby has had a rather bad reaction to our dinner." He turned to Mackaby. "Or perhaps it was my cigar?"

"Perhaps," whispered Mackaby, feeling his shame, his pain, his nearness to the black abyss of despair. He looked at Caroline, met her eyes for a heart beat, then turned away.

"James, are you all right?" she asked.

I will tell her, he thought. I will tell her . . . what? He turned back to where she stood, the embodiment of all he had ever dreamed of, ever loved. Caroline, David, his life, his lives. He tried to smell her perfume, but it mixed with the stench of his vomit, and he knew Harnish had won. He swallowed. "I'm fine, Mrs. Harnish. I think I should go home now."

Harnish's face relaxed. He shook Mackaby's hand. A show for Caroline, thought Mackaby. "A pity," Harnish said. "But I'm glad you could make it, Mackaby. I'll have Wilson show you out." With only a glance at Caroline, Harnish strode from the room.

Mackaby moved to the door but as he passed, Caroline took his hand. "James -- oh!" she gasped. He turned. Her eyes were large. Realizing he still held the watch in the hand she grasped, he wrenched it away. "I'm sorry," he cried. Stumbling through the banquet hall, he threw the watch on the table.

As Wilson held the door open, Mackaby looked back. Caroline sat at the dining table staring at him. She mouthed one word. He nodded. Tears streaming down his face, he left the house.

He limped down the long driveway wiping his hand against his coat again and again, the hand that had held the watch, as if to rub the stain of that night from his skin. As he walked, he whispered the word that Caroline had mouthed. A child's name. A child who now had never been. He whispered, "David."

#

Tick.

Holding the watch, she sits again at the table. Her husband sings upstairs, above the clatter of the servants washing dishes. She should have given the watch to her husband before he walked out the door tonight. But her husband had never been her husband. Her son had never been born.

Tick.

On the table lies a cake. Beside the cake lies a knife, long and sharp. She tries to read the writing in the icing of the cake, but the knife has cut pieces from it. It makes no sense. Her life . . . her lives make no sense. She knows she will never be able to put the pieces back together again, nor recall what they once said.

Tick.

Awakened, she lifts her head from the table. The banquet room is dark, the house silent except for the watch. She wonders why the servants did not rouse her. Perhaps they tried.

Rising, she climbs wide stairs, stands outside the bedroom door, hears the snoring of her husband. She steps inside, closing the door silently behind her. The man in bed is a stranger, yet she knows him. She thinks of James, of David. She thinks of the cake, her life, her lives. All is disorder.

Tick.

In one hand, she holds the watch. In the other, she clenches the knife from beside the cake. She walks to the bed.

Tick.

Pas De Deux

by Stephen Graham King

To drag himself from the shadow of that other guy, Stephen Graham King has dabbled at many things, from acting (most notably the Canadian premiere of "Noises Off"), to web design, blogging and graphic arts. Ironically, writing is the one thing that stuck. After relocating from Saskatoon to Toronto, Stephen began a career with Indigo Books and Music where he was responsible for writing company wide communications. When he can be dragged away from his computer for long enough, he can be found indulging his sick fascinations with crossword puzzles and home renovation shows on TLC (which is especially odd, considering his great fear of power tools). Stephen has recently published Just Breathe, the chronicle of his long battle against synovial sarcoma, from diagnosis through the various stages of treatment and surgeries. Online, Stephen can be found at *http://defyinggravity.ca*

I woke in the dark that morning
    Even in the years that the winters have been growing steadily longer and colder; steadily darker, it was unusual. When I opened my eyes there was usually grey morning light sneaking past the curtains behind my bed. But I hadn't gotten to sleep easily the night before.

That isn't unusual for me. When something unusual, something special is happening to me the next day, I toss and turn. The butterflies swarm my stomach, the "what if's" churn in my head, keeping sleep at bay. And this was a day that could change everything. This was no mere plane trip or new job.

As I lay there in the dark, I wasn't sure how long I had slept. The dark was so complete, so seamless, that it might have been minutes or hours. Without turning on a light, I fumbled to the night table for my watch or cell phone, whichever found its way into my palm first. It was the watch. I brought it close to my face (to compensate for the other genetic fault that plagued everyone in my family, our nearsightedness.) Pressing the button that lit the watch's face, I found that it was an hour or so before I had set my alarm to go off. It was another habit of mine. If I had no reason to get out of bed, I didn't. If there was something I needed to get up for, I would most likely wake several times before the set time, jerking awake in the certainty I had overslept.

Knowing I would never get back to sleep, I hunkered down under the sheet and duvet, wrapping myself against a coldness that wasn't entirely physical. In that dark and cool silence, I imagined I was actually aware of the cancer in my lungs; that I could feel it eating away at my body, subverting the processes of life. I was sure, lying there half awake and nestled in night's shadows, that I could feel the cells giving up, in those unlucky crapshoot locations that could not be reached by a surgeon without destroying my lungs' ability to actually breathe. I knew I was imagining it, knew it all too well. The first time I was diagnosed, I learned the truth all too quickly. Mostly, with cancer, you felt nothing until they began to treat you. Then the nausea, the weakness and excruciating pain from the surgeries began. That lesson has come fast and hard.

But not this time, they told me. This time would be different. If this worked, and they assured me there was a good chance it would, there would be no pain, no sickness. At least not for me.

I have always liked being in bed, liked the sensation of waking to the knowledge that I don't have to race to get out of bed, that I could stay there and just wait until I really want to get up. Even now, with this unknown day ahead of me, I could take a tiny grain of comfort in that. So, I lay there until the sensation of my body killing itself went away. Two more times I rolled over and checked my watch, rolling back over until my room began to lighten; before I gave up and threw the covers back. My legs waited by the bed, in the charger cradle that kept them powered while I slept. I reached for the left prosthesis, snapping it on and feeling the contacts on the inside warm slightly as they picked up the initial nerve impulses from the stump below my left knee. As I always did, I flexed the foot of the prosthesis (even now, I still can't refer to it as "my" foot). The nerve conduction system in the prosthesis gave me about 15 degrees of motion in the "ankle" Better than nothing, I guess, and better than they had 20 years ago. This slight degree of control was an achievement that had come only after long hours of biofeedback training to control the mechanism. I repeated the ritual with my right leg.

Slipping on my robe (funny how dressing had become a different routine. Put on the feet before putting on my clothes) I went to the bathroom and pissed, arching my back in a stretch. Then, with my bladder empty, I headed to the kitchen to make coffee.

When it was finished, I took my mug out to the balcony. It was cool that morning, and I pulled my robe tighter, but felt no need to put on a coat. It promised to be another of those warm autumn days. The leaves had started to turn, but only a few had begun to fall. There was a subtle glow in the east of the sun beginning to rise.

It's funny, in those quiet moments, when I am far from a hospital, that the memories come to me. I get wrapped up in thoughts of needles and tubes; of doctors and nurses. Of shitting into a bedpan and having my ass wiped by some stranger I have known only since her shift started. I remember again lying in the dark, pumping the PCA pump, waiting for the timed lockout to end and flood my body with narcotics; my leg one searing pain from the nerve grafts and the implantation of the leads to control the motion of the artificial leg. I remember puking my guts up for days from the post operative chemo.

Worst of all, I remembered all of those times I went back for checkups, hoping against hope that this time, everything would finally be done, that this time there would be no more spots on the scan of my chest. Unconsciously, I fingered the pink gnarl of scar tissue running down the middle of my chest, touching it like a talisman. It had been a neat seam once, barely visible. But that had been the first time. After the third or fourth time they had cut me open, the scar had begun to hypertrophy, growing thick and heavy as it healed. The light, gingery curls of hair on my chest did little to hide it. It made me mad, as the twin, wing-like scars on my back, where they had opened me to reach the tumours that they couldn't reach through my chest, were, in contrast, neat well healed lines, almost perfectly symmetrical. It was just my luck that they had become the almost attractive ones, the ones I could barely see.

It's in the quiet times that those memories come out to play. Like the day they told me the cancer had returned yet again, this time inoperable. That afternoon I'd thought I was okay with it, that I had fought the good fight and was more than ready to throw down my hand and step away from the table. But when they had come to me a few weeks later proposing this radical new procedure, something broke in me, surprising me and shaking me. I found myself eagerly agreeing before I knew what I was saying. I don't think I even really listened to them as they outlined the details, the risks. Something in me fell profoundly in love with the idea of staying alive, of not letting the bastard disease take me. The feeling surprised me. I thought I had made peace with the thought of dying, that the years of treatments had eroded my resistance, my will. But I had been wrong. The patina had worn away to reveal something steely underneath. In that instant, I would have done anything, sacrificed anything for more time, for more life.

I sat there, sipping my coffee while the thoughts danced around my head.

Why me? There was no more an answer now than on the day I had been originally diagnosed. Now, though, in this context, on the morning of this day when I and he and the doctors would supposedly make history, there was another facet of the incomplete answer.

Why me? Because my genes sufficiently matched his. Because my DNA passed the rigorous tests that the researchers deemed necessary for the experimental treatment to proceed.

I turned my back on the sunrise and went back inside, drawn to the spot where I spent much of my time now whenever I was home. I poured myself more coffee and went into the room that was my office. It was untidier than usual, books in unkempt piles, newspapers and magazines sprouting sticky tabs that marked articles to be read or clipped out. Just walking into the room, I felt the arguments and rebuttals in all the written words pressing against me, peering at me from the wall behind my desk.

The original bulletin board had been centred neatly on the wall behind my desk, (my once need for parallel lines had caused me to carefully measure the wall to ensure the spacing) but it had become so full of clippings and articles that I had needed to add another one. Some of the newspaper cuttings had begun to yellow and curl at the edges, where they took the light from the window. Others were pieces I had found online and printed out. Some were glossy, taken from magazines. Here and there, some relevant thought had been circled or highlighted in fluorescent yellow. Every clipping had comments scrawled in blue ink, by my hand stuffed into the margins. On the desk below the cork board was the most recent stack of books I had accumulated: the life stories and true crime books that had been written in the wake of his capture.

Gustav "Gus" Pike. 44 at the time of his arrest outside of Orillia. Killer of 15 boys and girls between the ages of 6 and 10 before the police had finally caught up with him, finding a mass grave filled with a confusion of underdeveloped bones. The RCMP chief heading the investigation who had come off so burly and hard in the days of the investigation, wept on camera after the grave had been found. I remember following the trial on TV, like everyone else did, growing more horrified as further details came to light of the ongoing sexual assaults before the eventual murders. But I had to admit I was horrified in that detached way, never dreaming that his life would somehow intersect with mine. I knew none of the victims or their families. As the world had grown morally colder, we had all grown inured to stories like this one. But even so, there was something more resonant about this case. Maybe it was the public mood, just one of those rare congruencies of time, person and circumstance or maybe it was the savagery of the murders. Who knows, maybe we were tired of the increasing diet of death and destruction on our news, but the public outcry for Gus Pike's punishment was loud and bloodthirsty.

Who knew that his punishment would be this?

I looked at his pictures, everything from his mug shot to the candid snapshots that people in his life had eagerly offered up as sacrifices to the media. In his mug shot, he looked haggard and drawn, haunted by something from his own past. His features blunt and ugly. As the trial progressed, we all learned about the abuse he had suffered, but remained somehow unmoved. There was something hard and unapologetic about him as we watched him in court, something unyielding even on the day of the verdict. Maybe if he had shown some sign of remorse, maybe if he had been somehow more photogenic, the cries for his blood might not have rung so loudly.

But if the calls for justice or vengeance had not been so strident, we wouldn't be where we were. I wouldn't have this slim, potentially golden chance.

Originally, I wasn't supposed to know who he was, wasn't to know that he would be the one. The donor would be anonymous and I would merely be at the hospital to receive the treatment once the sentence had been carried out. It was foolishly naive of them to think that they could keep it from me. The press and the civil liberties lawyers would have none of it. My face was all over the papers and so was his. The media revelled in reliving the details of his crimes and his eventual capture, splashing picture after picture of the tiny bodies and the basement littered with underdeveloped bones. His trial was the trial of the century, followed across the country. When he was sentenced, it was a verdict heard around the world.

And today the sentence would be carried out.

When my coffee was gone, I showered, as I knew the car would be arriving to take me to the Hospital. My small bag was packed and ready, and I was dressed and at the door when my bell rang.

The car was black and, I knew, armoured. Since Doctor Feinstein had been shot and killed outside his home, security had drawn ever tighter, even at the checkpoints along University and College. The guards, wrapped in black coats, ushered me into the back seat and closed the doors. I head a thunk as the doors locked me in and we pulled away from the curb. There wasn't much traffic or activity at this time of the morning, something that had changed a lot in the years since I was a kid. The curfew had changed much of that. The mumble of traffic and the sirens that I had heard all the time as I was growing up had grown quieter and quieter. Now, there were almost no cars along Queen Street, the shops and street corners all ghostly quiet. What little traffic there was moved much faster now that the streetcars had all been taken out of service, when they became too expensive to maintain. Now all that remained were the rusting tracks embedded in the pavement. There were only buses on the streets now, their windows heavily shielded against stray bullets, jostling Toronto's commuters like armoured cocktail shakers.

The car turned north onto University and we passed the construction site where the U.S. Embassy once was. Some developer was finally building there, after the bombing back in '14. People had been superstitious about that bit of land for a long time. Most felt that was when things started going bad for Toronto. Not me. Once I got sick, my definition of bad luck changed a lot.

We were moving north on University, heading straight for the entrance to the parking garage at Elm street, where all the Hospitals had grown together, overtaking the section of the street leading to what had once been Queen's Park. The massive Central Research Hospital, which had once been four separate hospitals, loomed in the windshield, like a bridge spanning the lanes of University Avenue. When the U.S. had moved against all reproductive technologies in their moral majority Jihad, closing abortion clinics and amending the constitution to ban cloning, stem cell research and severely limiting medical research, the steady outflow of Canada's best research minds suddenly reversed. The decades long Brain Drain changed its flow and Canadian research hospitals were suddenly flooded with the minds and the dollars to surge forward. Canny fundraisers and entrepreneurs saw the chance and took it, building what would become one of the leading research hospitals in the world.

Which was practically my second home, my latest dysfunctional, Love-Hate relationship. I always felt a little on edge as I approached this monolith of a building, but it wasn't the sight that was setting me on edge today. It took a second to realize that it was sound, a low rumble of voices; agitated, angry. Then I saw them.

Lining University, from Dundas north to the Hospital, was a huge mass of people, pressed against barricades at the sidewalks. As we got closer, I could see the placards and handmade signs; could see the restless, angry waves passing through the mob. At the checkpoint outside the hospital, I watched as the guard lifted my card, stamped with the hospital stamp to the window when it lowered. One black-gloved hand took it from another, then returned it, waving the driver on.

I wondered if Louise Crane was somewhere in the crowd. I couldn't imagine her missing this day. It had been her victim impact statement, made with a fierce, dignified grief on behalf of all the parents that Gus Pike had taken children from, that had swayed the judge and jury most. She was the lightning rod that had galvanized public opinion. She was the one that had researched the changes in the laws that allowed families of victims of violent crimes to move beyond merely expressing their loss to actually influencing sentencing. When the voices of the devastated parents were heard at Pike's sentencing, Louise was the one speaking the words. She was the one calling for some faint redemption to his life, some purpose to his death. No, Louise wouldn't have missed this day.

As the car moved forward, somewhere ahead one of the metal barricades gave way and the crowd surged out in one sudden, angry impulse. In the windshield, I saw the bodies spill forth in a wave against the hood of the car, filling my vision with angry shouting faces. Placards slammed against the hood, the fenders, the side windows; then were followed by gloved hands, some open and slapping, others closed into rigid fists. The angry rumble swelled into a roar, like an earthquake or a heavy wave breaking against the shore. Around me, the car vibrated with it, setting my teeth further on edge. The glass by my face was suddenly full of angry faces and I shifted back in my seat, flinching from a wave of hatred that I could actually feel on my skin.

I shivered and pulled my coat closer around me. I don't care what anyone says about not caring what others think of you. I defy anyone to remain unmoved in the face of that mob. In a sudden shift, I felt a flash of anger. To these people, my lingering death from cancer was acceptable. But Gus Pike's execution for crimes that made even the strongest souls sick with horror, which would most likely keep me alive; that was a heinous societal evil. The voice behind my eyes wanted to scream at them, pound back at the glass. Fuck you all. I will not lose my life for a killer of children.

Just as quickly as the crowd had surged at the car, the riot police waded in and began the slow push to get them back under control. We began to move slowly forward again. There was another security checkpoint at the maw of the parking garage and there was more showing of IDs and comparing of papers. I waited. After the initial candidate for this experiment had been gunned down outside her house and I had become the one, I had no objections to anything that might have kept me alive.

When the car stopped outside the elevator, my bodyguards swept the area outside the elevator to make sure it was safe. They pushed the button and waited, keeping me in the car until the doors actually opened and they were sure that the elevator was empty. Then, in a hustle of activity, swift and economical, my door was opened and I was in the elevator.

Up on the 12th floor, Rosie, the nurse was waiting for me and she smiled when she saw me. We were old comrades in arms, Rosie and me. She had tended me during the surgeries, measured my vitals in the night. She was the one who talked to me when I was freaked out or scared. Now she was the one that would prep me for the procedure to come. I felt the agitation drain from me as I looked in her deep, dark eyes; saw her white teeth against her brown skin. Speaking in gentle, lightly accented tones, she led me to the bed and gave me a gown to change into, then pulled the curtain around the bed.

I hate those gowns; I think they are designed to torture us. As if patients have not suffered enough, they must take away every shred of our dignity. I took off my clothes and folded them neatly, slipping on the worn, rumpled cotton gown, tying the strings closed as best I could to cover myself. I climbed onto the bed and raised the head so I was sitting upright.

Rosie came back a few minutes later, carrying a plastic basket with medical supplies, to find me whistling, off key and tuneless. She pulled back the curtain and placed the basket down on the table.

"Ready then?" she asked, taking my hand and probing for a vein. They always had trouble finding a vein now. Too many years of IVs and chemo had traumatized my veins and left even the simple process of drawing blood an involved procedure. She placed the rubber tourniquet around my arm and tightened it, reaching into the basket. She frowned, obviously struggling to find a usable vein, finally giving up and moving to the other arm.

As she retied the tourniquet, the door opened and a young man in scrubs, maybe a cleaner or an orderly came in. Behind him in the hallway, I saw a group of people outside the door. He must have seen them too, for he stopped to watch them go by.

It was really a freak coincidence that I saw him. The orderly in the doorway was positioned in such a way and the door was open and my curtain was drawn back, something stopped the entourage just outside the door. Rosie was too preoccupied to notice.

I recognized the bright orange of his coverall as being out of place in the halls of an urban hospital. It was only then that I noticed the heavy shackles binding his hands and feet. Standing there, his head turned in my direction and his eyes locked with mine.

In his pale eyes, watery and bloodshot, I saw something empty and cold, something like a bleak night in late autumn just before the first snow falls; when there is nothing left alive. It was the feeling that had come on me in the nights, those dark nights during the first round of treatment when I would have given anything for the sick, queasy dread to go away. In those blank, expressionless eyes were a thousand deaths: the one I was about to cheat; the sudden endings of the dozens of young lives he had brutally taken. I saw the death that was coming to him.

Capital punishment by forced altruism.

The mutagenic cocktail would be administered, further bringing his DNA in line with mine. Then, he would be injected with a cultured mix of cells from my tumour and accelerants to ensure it took hold rapidly. After that would come the magic bullet, the new experimental immunogen that was the whole point of this process. He would sicken quickly and horribly, and as he died, his body would produce monoclonal antibodies specifically designed to attack the cancer cells. These would be transfused into me and cure me of the cancer once and for all. At least that was the theory. Louise and the other parents of those children he had killed would have their tiny sliver of comfort. And I would have my life back.

The glance lasted only a moment. I don't know if he knew who I was as nothing seemed to register on his face. I looked away for a moment as Rosie announced that she had a vein. There was a sharp second of pain as needle punctured my skin and when I looked back, he was gone.

The Identity Factor

by Andrew Weiner

Andrew Weiner has had more
than 50 short stories published in
magazines and newspapers, has also
been translated into French, Italian,
Czech, Polish and Japanese, and
has had short stories filmed for two
different television programs. His
most recent novel, Getting Near The
End has been hailed as a sharply
sardonic and superbly crafted novel.
Weiner holds an M. Sc in social
psychology from the London School
of Economics and lives in Toronto
with his wife Barbara Moses.

"The Identity Factory" originally appeared in Science Fiction Age, *January 1999*

1.

Lou Grendel first heard about the Identity Factory from his cousin Mel, when he called from the airport to cancel their squash game.

"Can't make it," he said. "I'm going mountain climbing in the Himalayas."

"Mountain climbing? But you're afraid of heights."

You're afraid of your own shadow, he wanted to say, but held back.

"That's true enough," Mel said. "Or at least, it *was* true. I was afraid of heights, and almost everything else. The old me was a cringing coward, afraid to face life's challenges. But that's all over with. The new me is brave and strong and powerful."

Lou held the phone further away from his ear. At the very least, Mel *sounded* different: usually soft-spoken and tentative, he was now loud and forceful, if not to say downright bombastic.

"What's up, Mel? You on Prozac or something?"

"Better. I've been to the Identity Factory."

"The where?"

"It's the new thing, Lou. And I got in on the ground floor. Soon everyone is going to be getting themselves a whole new identity."

"Oh, I get it," Lou said. "Kind of like the Witness Protection Program."

"You've got a good sense of humor, Lou. But sometimes you hide behind it, shutting out anything that's new and scary. I'm sure you don't mind me telling you that."

"Feel free."

"You might want to see a dentist about your gums, too. They look like they're receding."

Lou wasn't sure that he liked the new, more forceful Mel.

"Anything else that's been bothering you?"

"Plenty, but we can catch up later. The point is, this Identity Factory thing works. I've been through it all . . . analysis, Gestalt, Rolfing, EST, NLP, TM, channeling, dream work. None of it really helped. This one does. You become who you really want to be."

"But how . . .?"

"Gotta go, Lou, they're calling my flight. But you'll be hearing plenty about it soon, you bet."

2.

Lou heard more about the Identity Factory the very next day.

He had just finished screening the last segment of *The Manchurian Candidate* for his PopCult 101 section. He screened old movies as often as he could. It got him off his feet, it let him slip out to his office to make a few calls or take a nap when he was feeling really beat. And the students liked it, too. No one could say that Lou had not learned a trick or two in coasting through ten years as a community college lecturer.

Today he had hoped to use the movie to lead a review of conspiracy *motifs* in American popular culture from the Kennedy assassination through to the *X Files*. But his students mostly wanted to talk about how the Lawrence Harvey character had been brainwashed by his Red Chinese captors and transformed into an assassination weapon.

"Is that really possible," asked a worried-looking blond girl in the front row. "To change someone's personality like that? Like flipping a switch?"

Lou shrugged. "You'd have to ask your psych professor. Although personally I don't think it's possible."

"What about Patty Hearst?" someone asked.

"That's a good point. Maybe we should take a look at the Schrader movie . . ."

"What about the Identity Factory?" asked the worried-looking girl. "You know, that new place they're advertising on the radio where they change your life in seven days, satisfaction guaranteed or your money refunded."

Lou frowned slightly. This was getting off the point, but he was interested despite himself.

"I heard something about that."

"Our next door neighbor went to become more assertive. Now she's become a lesbian and she's moving to Yellowknife."

"Why Yellowknife?" Lou couldn't help but ask. But the student didn't know.

3.

That night, Lou went for dinner at his sister Audrey's house. Audrey was married to Max, who owned a paint supply store downtown. Lou liked his sister and her husband well enough, and he was not usually one to pass up a free meal. But he tried to avoid eating at Audrey's, because she was such a terrible cook. Which was probably why Max was rail-thin. Lou had tried to duck out of this dinner, too, but Audrey had been insistent, hinting at important news.

As it turned out, dinner was spectacular. Starting out with broiled shrimps in coconut sauce, moving through a three-leaf salad and a palate-cleansing lemon sherbet to stuffed quail and *crème brulee*, it was all delicious.

"This is great, Audrey," Lou said. "Outstanding."

"I wish I could take the credit," Audrey said. "But it was Max."

"Max?" Lou turned to stare at his brother-in-law in astonishment. "I didn't know you could cook."

"Couldn't boil an egg," Max said. "But now I can, thanks to the Identity Factory. In fact I'm selling the store and opening a restaurant."

"But why?"

"I was doing all right," Max said. "Great wife, wonderful kids, a nice house, a good business. But always there was something . . . *missing*. Then I read a flier about this new Identity Factory. So I went down to hear what they had to say. And I decided to give it a try. They gave me a bunch of tests. And it turned out that I ought to be a chef."

"But even so," Lou said, "how do you become an expert chef overnight?"

"First you have a little operation," Max said, pulling back his right ear to reveal a tiny socket.

Lou recoiled. "They drill a hole in your head?"

"Just a little one. Local anesthetic. Then you plug in the program. You can buy off-the-shelf, or have one customized. And it gives you what you need. I have the skills, the recipes and the confidence of a topflight *cordon bleu* chef."

"What's it like?" Lou asked. "Being someone else?"

"Oh, I'm still me. Underneath, I'm still *me*."

Whoever that was, Lou thought, staring uneasily at his happy, flushed and noticeably-more-plump brother-in-law. Because he didn't know this person at all.

4.

After dinner, Lou went over to Marie's apartment. Marie taught Woman's Studies at the college where he worked. They had been seeing each other for a while, although it was nothing intense. He had invited Marie to accompany him to Audrey's house, but she had preferred to stay home watch a feminist British detective show on PBS.

"What kind of a world is this?" Lou asked, after he had told Marie about Max. "Where someone would do something like that?"

"Why wouldn't they?" Marie asked. "It's the next logical step, after all. People buy clothes, cars, houses to reflect who they are, or want to be. I mean, every second staff member at college drives a Volvo, because they think it's professorial or something. Why stop there? Why not go out and buy a personality, too? "

"But it's not the same thing," he protested. "To give up your personality, your individuality, your dignity as a human being . . ."

"Maybe Max never had much of a personality to begin with. Besides, you said he was unhappy. Unfulfilled."

"Unhappy!" He snorted. "Who said he was supposed to be happy? Whoever said that was part of the deal?"

5.

Lou's Deadhead friend, Al, was the next to go.

Al worked as a dispatcher for a courier company. But he lived for the Grateful Dead. He spent endless hours logging on to Usenet discussion groups. Trading tapes around the world, he had amassed thousands of hours of live Dead performances. Since the death of Jerry Garcia and the dissolution of the group he had if anything become even more fanatical in his completism.

Lou didn't have quite the same enthusiasm. But he liked to dabble, and had accumulated a small tape collection of his own. Once or twice a month he would visit with Al and a couple of his other Deadhead friends and they would get stoned -- Al always had the best grass -- and play some new tapes.

"Hey Al," Lou said, when he called to confirm the next get-together. "We still on for Friday? I just picked up this terrific early performance of 'Viola Lee Blues' . . ."

"Well actually," Al said, and his voice was strained, "I was going to call you about that. You see, I've got tickets for a show that night."

"Oh," Lou said. "I didn't know anyone interesting was in town."

"Tony Bennett," Al said. "I'm going to see Tony Bennett."

"Oh," Lou said. "Well, that's cool, I guess. Maybe next Friday then."

"Actually I was going to see Billy Joel."

"You kidding me, Al?"

"No. I know it sounds strange, but it's like my ears have been opened to other kinds of music. I've realized that there's more to life than the Dead. In fact, since I went to the Identity Factory, I can't even listen to them anymore. Which is just as well, since I really don't have much free time, now that I'm working for my real estate license."

"*You* went to the Identity Factory? But why, Al? Why?"

"Because I was wasting my life, that's why."

"And selling real estate is an improvement?"

"People need houses, Lou. It's a shelter *and* an investment, the best you can make. In fact, this is a terrific time to get in on the market, what with interest rates being so low ..."

6.

His ex-wife Charlotte called. They hadn't spoken in two years, and the last occasion had been a screaming match at her lawyer's office.

At first, Lou was suspicious. What more does she want of me, he wondered? I have no more. But as it turned out, she wanted to give.

"I wanted to say goodbye," she said, "and to forgive you."

"Forgive me? You were the one who was screwing around."

"Only because you drove me to it by being so emotionally distant and ungiving. But there's two sides to every story and if I was at fault I offer you my heartfelt apologies."

In all the years he had known her, Charlotte had never apologized for anything.

"I also wanted to let you know that I'm sending you a check. I'm repaying your settlement. I don't need the money, and I've transcended my petty economic insecurities."

"Are you feeling alright, Charlotte?"

"Never better. I'm leaving for India tomorrow, to work with lepers."

"Let me guess. You went to the Identity Factory."

"And became the generous person I always wanted to be. How about you, Lou? Thinking of trying it?"

"I'm fine just the way I am."

"Teaching cultural studies in community college? Come on Lou. There must have been *something* you really wanted to do. Write. Paint. Make films."

"Not really."

"You want more, Lou. You're just to afraid to admit it, even to yourself."

"I like my life just the way it is," he told her.

He thought of himself as a pretty good teacher, all things considered. Maybe he was a little too easygoing. Maybe he didn't inspire his students. But at least he kept most of them awake, most of the time, which was as much as you could really hope for.

Oh, sure, he had once had other dreams. He had wanted to make films, or at least write film criticism. Teaching college had just been a stopgap. But the years had gone by, and he never had done anything else. Which suggested that he had never really wanted to anything else.

And still, he couldn't help wondering if Charlotte might be right.

7.

Driving home from work, Lou heard a commercial for the Identity Factory. They were holding free public presentations in a hotel near the airport, every hour on the hour. *"Learn about the new process that is about to change your world . . . New identities from $399.95. All major credit cards accepted."*

It was strange, he thought, the way this Identity Factory had suddenly appeared from nowhere. Spooky, almost, like some kind of secret alien invasion . . . like in Carpenter's *They Live*, or something. But most likely it was just capitalism as usual.

It was a scam, anyway. Just another fad, another cult, another McTherapy, another way of milking hapless, brainwashed consumers of their hard-earned savings.

But then again, what if it worked?

What if it really worked?

8.

Marie called as he walked in the door. "I'm going to the Identity Factory presentation at 9.00," she told him. "Want to come with?"

"You're not serious?"

"I want to find out what this is about."

"You'll never come back," he said. "You'll go off to become a water ski instructor in Bali."

"I don't necessarily plan to *do* anything. I want to explore my options."

"But you love teaching."

"Not all the time," she said. "And it's not just a matter of my work. It's my whole life. Maybe I want to have kids, or run for office, or travel round the world."

Lou felt a sudden panic. Not Marie, too.

"Can't you see," he said desperately, "it's society that's doing this to you? Making you dissatisfied with your life. So that you run out to buy something, consume something."

"Save it for your section on culture-jamming, Lou. I'm going. How about you?"

"They're showing Kiss Me Deadly on channel 19. It's the culmination of film noir."

"You can tape it," she said. "Or not."

9.

The speaker on the stage paced back and forth, tiger-like, trailing the cord of his hand-held microphone, radiating good health and personal dynamism. He was lean and bronzed and dressed in an expensive-looking silver-gray suit. He wore a white mandarin collar shirt with no tie.

The speaker's name was Calvin Hudson. Or so he claimed. It sounded a little made-up to Lou.

"Freedom of choice," Hudson was saying. "Choose your own

personality. Be charming or sly, aggressive or sexy. Be whoever you want to be."

Lou shifted uncomfortably on the folding metal chair and nibbled on a stale doughnut. Beside him, Marie sat in rapt attention.

"Be left-handed or right-handed, Russian or American, a tycoon or a thief . . ."

The room was packed. It was hot and stuffy and smelled faintly of stale farts. Lou couldn't wait to get out. But he had promised Marie to keep an open mind.

"You ever hear of a lady called Sybil?" the speaker asked. "You ever wondered how she did that? How she could be so many different people at once? What is a multiple personality disorder, really? I'll tell you what it is. It's *self-programming*, that's what it is. It's deciding to be somebody else. And that's exactly what you're going to do. Except, unlike Sybil, you won't have to do it all yourself, because we're going to help you."

After the speech, Hudson invited the audience to come upfront to sign up for some "identity work."

"Absolutely no risk, folks," he told them. "All our work comes with a complete guarantee. Money back if not completely satisfied."

The audience stood up as if as one, and began to file towards the front. Marie stood up too, as if to follow them.

"Marie," he said, putting his hand on her arm. "Don't you want to go home? We can still catch the beginning of Letterman."

"I'm going to sign up," she said. Her face was set, determined. "Don't try to stop me."

Something in her gaze made him release her arm.

Watching the crowd shuffling forward eagerly reminded him, inescapably, of the last scene of Segal's *Invasion Of The Bodysnatchers*.

He fled the room.

10.

"Not signing-up?" said the voice from the shadows, as Lou stepped from the hotel into the parking lot. "Could I ask why not?"

He turned to see Calvin Hudson, a cigarette cupped in his hand.

"You smoke?" Lou asked, surprised at this apparent display of weakness.

"Only on Wednesdays," Hudson said. "It's under control. So tell me . . . what's your name?"

"Lou."

"Tell me, Lou . . . please call me Cal, by the way . . . is it the price?" He leaned forward, apparently keenly interested.

"The price seems fair enough. If that's what someone wants. And if you can really deliver it."

"Oh, we deliver it, don't doubt it. But you don't want it?"

"No," Lou said. "It's just not for me."

"Why not?"

"What do you care what I think?"

"That's what we're here for, Lou," Hudson said. "Information." He dropped his cigarette butt on the ground and trod in it. "This is just the pilot phase. We're here to learn everything we can about what works and what doesn't before we roll out nationally."

"Identity Factories in every city?"

"On every block. And we've got a whole world to conquer. This is a bottomless market, Lou. These days, everyone's confused. No one is happy, no one is satisfied. No one knows who the hell they're supposed to be anymore. People are desperate for something like this."

Lou shivered. "Where are you people from? Mars?"

"I'm from Chicago myself." He looked at Lou appraisingly. "So tell me, what's not to like about a new, improved you?"

"I don't know . . . It's just so *packaged*. I mean, I always thought of myself as an individualist, you know. Not a conformist."

"*Individualist*," Hudson echoed, mockingly. "*Conformist*. Words. Meaningless words. Outdated concepts. *This* is the true individualism. Wake up Lou, you're living in modern times now."

"But to change your whole personality . . ."

"Don't we all try to be something we're not? The difference is, now you don't have to act anymore. Now you can *be* who you want to be for real."

"But I don't . . ."

"Don't what?"

Lou shook his head. "I don't know what I want."

Hudson shook his head. "You may think you don't know.

But actually you do. And we can help you get in touch with it. You want to be a big business tycoon? A babe magnet? A TV star? A super salesperson? We can give you the personality traits, the knowledge, the self-confidence . . . the rest is up to you."

"And I'd be happy?"

"Absolutely."

"But I wouldn't be me anymore."

"Isn't that the whole point? I mean, with all due respect, Lou, is it so great being you?"

"Maybe it's not so great," Lou said. "But isn't that what Kierkegaard said? To live is to be anxious? Something like that."

Hudson was shaking his head from side-to-side. "Don't you ever get tired, always questioning yourself and everything else? Wouldn't you like things clear and simple for once? Wouldn't you like to be sure who you really are?"

"And Freud," Lou continued, "he said the natural state of the mature human being was a qualified unhappiness . . . Or was that F. Scott Fitzgerald?"

"Just listen to yourself, Lou," Hudson said. "I mean, really listen for a moment. And then tell me you wouldn't rather be someone else."

Lou stood and thought for a long moment.

"I can make you happy," Hudson said. "Trust me."

And suddenly he gave in.

"Alright," he said. "Give it your best shot."

11.

Marie called the next day to apologize.

"I'm sorry for rushing off like that the other night. I don't know what got into me."

"Don't worry about it."

"I feel like such an idiot," Marie said. "You know, I actually went through their idiotic tests. They had this whole program worked out for me. If you can believe it, I was going to quit my job and work part-time as a cocktail waitress while writing romance novels."

"Well," Lou said, "you would look good in one of those short skirts. And I always thought you had a hidden romantic streak."

"They really had me going for a moment," she said. "But I came to my senses at the last moment. You were right, Lou. You were right all along. Anyway, I guess I'll see you at college."

"You bet."

12.

Lou was watering his bonsai tree and listening to an Enya CD when Calvin Hudson came to call. He put down his watering can and turned down the music and opened the door.

"How you feeling?" Hudson asked.

Lou raised his hand and touched the implant behind his ear. It itched slightly, but otherwise appeared to be completely healed.

"Good," he said.

"And the program?"

"Running good

"But you had some questions?"

"Yes," Lou said. "I appreciate you coming by."

"Like I told you, Lou, this is about information. We need to know what works and what doesn't. So if you're unhappy, I want to know that."

"Actually I've been feeling pretty good. It's just that I expected a little *more*."

"More what?" Hudson asked, taking a cigarette pack out of his pocket and looking around for an ashtray. "Mind if I smoke, by the way?"

"Yes I do mind," Lou said, fussily. "Second-hand smoke kills, you know that. Besides, this is Tuesday."

Hudson put the pack away. "It's under control," he said. "You were saying, you expected more."

"More change," Lou said. "I mean, some things are different. I suddenly have this interest in bonsai, and making my own wine, and going to basketball games. But I'm still a college teacher."

"And you're not enjoying life?"

"I'm enjoying it. But it's, I don't know, kind of *dull*."

"It's what the tests told us Lou. Sometimes it just turns out that way. You find out that you're already what you ought to be, with maybe a little fine-tuning."

"I guess I was hoping for something a little more exciting. Like a test pilot. Or maybe a movie director."

Hudson shook his head sadly. "It wouldn't work. It would conflict with your underlying personality structures, ultimately producing trauma." He got to his feet. "But if you don't like the results of our work, we can take it out and offer you a full refund."

Lou stared over at his bonsai, which was beginning to take shape. The radio was playing a particularly good Enya track. Over by the window, the papers for next year's course plans were spread out on his desk. He had always winged it before, but was looking forward to taking a more methodical approach. With a little more work, he could be a better teacher, perhaps even an inspiring teacher.

Besides, he had tickets for the Raptors game tonight. Tomorrow he was going over to Al's to listen to some Mel Torme tapes. And next week he was taking delivery on his new Volvo.

"No," he said. "I think I'll try it for awhile longer."

Shadows

by Karen Danylak

> Karen Danylak is a Toronto-based
> speculative fiction writer. When she's
> not writing, she works as a marketing
> manager for a mutual fund company
> in Toronto's financial district. She
> lives with her husband and a crazy
> black cat named Max.

Quiet as a mouse. Must stay quiet as a mouse.

If I'd been able to move my lips, they would have been mouthing my litany, but I had to stay still and silent and hidden in the darkest place I could imagine.

The Pleurgen tech standing in front of me poked and prodded my flesh a few more times then shrugged his shoulders.

"Ms. Sheung," he addressed the vid screen on the wall behind me, "I've run all the standard diagnostics and I can't find anything wrong with your proxy."

Catherine clambered roughly into my head, surging down the link.

"It figures," my mouth said. "It never acts up when a tech is around. Are you sure there aren't any more tests you can run? None of my other proxies ever experienced response lags like this one does."

The tech finger-combed his thinning hair and grimaced. "I'd have to take it back to the lab, Ms. Sheung."

Not the lab, not the lab. My mantra changed as I fought off panic. I remembered what they had done to defectives at the Pleurgen labs before I had been sold. Why grow more raw material when you could recycle? The only safe thing was to hide.

"No. I can't do without a proxy for that long," Catherine

said.

That's right, you can't, Catherine, I thought. When the link was active I could see into her mind. She'd never leave the safety of her house and no one would deliver the type of merchandise Catherine liked.

"If that's all then, Ms. Sheung," the tech said, "I really have to go if I'm going to make it through *decontam* and get to my next call on time."

"Fine." She waved my hand with the casual dismissiveness of the very rich. "If I have any more problems, I'll be in touch."

I relaxed a fraction as the tech left my storage shed. This was the second time in a month Catherine had had me checked out. It was only a matter of time before she decided to replace me. I'd been too bold, too interested in preserving the little spark of life I had. I'd let my thoughts float far enough into the foreground that they'd interfered with Catherine's control.

Proxies weren't supposed to have minds of their own. We were the biological version of bots, a safe way for the wealthy to experience a dangerous world. My existence was no great shakes but when it was threatened, I held on to it with a death grip.

Once the tech was gone, we jumped in Catherine's car, punching in the route program with practiced ease. Catherine needed her fix.

The car purred to life and headed to the first security checkpoint.

"Vid on. News," Catherine ordered.

A local Ananova came to life on the screen, reading the news in clipped tones. "…and Pleurgen Biotech announced this morning that it anticipates filling ten thousand orders for their model 9C proxies using its rapid growth process next quarter. In related news, next month will mark the twentieth anniversary of the 2021 attacks in Toronto. The perfect storm of terrorist activity caused the death of thousands and forced the eventual abandonment of Toronto's financial district. The…"

"Off!" Catherine snapped. She hated reminders of the attacks. I hated her memories of them, of the bodies twitching spasmodically in the streets as their nervous systems shut down; of the bombed out buildings and the poisoned air.

Last month I'd gotten a first hand taste. Catherine had sent us to an underground club. Well hidden, or so the patrons thought. But people gathered together attract them like sharks to blood. I don't know who set off the car bomb. Every marginalized group in the world had blended into a continuum of rage that lashed out without warning.

I'd been lucky, I suppose, heading out the back door into an alley when the blast went off. I woke a few hours later, lying on the pavement a hundred meters away, blood oozing from an assortment of scrapes and cuts. Catherine's mind was gone, fled to the safety of her own body and her protected house. All around me were proxies, abandoned shells unable to cry out in pain at their injuries. One of them was on fire, burning to death and unable to save himself. They were empty.

I lay there for hours, playing proper proxy. Defectives were terminated. The only safe thing was to hide. But each minute that ticked away brought a new level of horror as I wondered if there was worse to come. Plain vanilla bombs weren't in fashion anymore. They usually came with extras like VX or radiation pellets.

Just when I thought Catherine might have written me off, her mind flowed back down the link. Most people would have abandoned an injured proxy but she wanted the meth we had bought in the club and I had it. The irony wasn't lost on me that the addictions that had sent me into danger were my salvation that day. But since then I'd grown warier, less able to control the instinct to act on my own.

The car glided to a halt at the perimeter of the Core. We had to walk the rest of the way. Bay Street was its usual gloomy self, the streets strewn with trash and rubble. The skeleton of a bombed out building at the corner of Adelaide cut a jagged path through the sky. But the street was reassuringly empty, the only other being on the street a tarnished bot.

Catherine loved sending me into the Core. It was a safe thrill, the only danger to her the inconvenience of losing another proxy. It was also the best part of town to get stuff you couldn't order over the Net.

We entered one of the intact buildings a bit further south, at King Street, and walked down a frozen escalator into the tunnels below.

My eyes blinked, adjusting to the shadows, the only lights those that enterprising squatters and Core merchants had managed to jury-rig to a power source. Catherine's memories intruded again – she had worked in one of the towers above before the attacks of '21, had shopped in the stores below when the halls were a teeming mass of bright lights and life. I always found it hard to reconcile her memories with the dingy reality. It seemed too terrifying that so many people would congregate in a single place.

She walked us over to the usual store. Once the place had been called LCBO, but the original sign had fallen months ago and now leaned against a wall inside, the letters cracked and warped. The place still sold much the same merchandise as it once had, but the current occupant kept some more exotic products in stock.

Proxies and bots dotted the store, all surveying the thin selection of dusty bottles spread on the shelves. Titus, the shopkeeper, perched on a stool behind the counter and watched with a sour look on his pock-marked face. His only concession to safety was an old style gas mask that hung around his skinny neck.

I smiled inside as I saw one of the proxies who frequented Titus's shop almost as often as we did. He was slim and blond with long fingers that caressed the curves of the bottle he held. Sometimes I amused myself by imagining that he was like me, trapped inside an owner-controlled body. My ogling was cut short; Catherine had no interest in flesh. Her cravings were intensifying. I could feel them vibrating down the link like an over-tuned guitar string being plucked.

We walked over to Titus. "What's today's special?" Catherine asked.

"I have some Cubans and a few crystals." He pulled a grimy shoebox from under the counter and lifted the lid to reveal some crumbly cigars and three small chunks of crystal in a vial.

"I'll take the meth."

"Two hundred cred," he said flatly.

"One hundred hard," Catherine countered.

Titus sucked his teeth but held out his hand and we slapped a roll of five dollar coins into it then pocketed the vial.

When the blast went off above ground, I felt it more than I heard it, a deep boom that resonated in my chest. Then the rumbling began, the death song of a building stressed beyond tolerance. Catherine fled back along the link, leaving me before she had to experience anything distasteful.

I leapt over the counter and crouched beneath its flimsy protection with Titus, who had pulled the gas mask up on his face. Dust and chunks of ceiling rained down; something big above ground must have gotten hit. As I cowered next to Titus, I couldn't make myself fall limp like a normal proxy should.

When the dust settled and the rumbling stopped, I pulled myself up from behind the counter. The store was darker. Two of the lights had broken and the others were buzzing and flickering, casting eerie shadows. Puddles of alcohol and broken glass littered the floor. The bots stood silently; the other proxies lay in limp heaps on the ground like discarded rag dolls. And the door was choked with rubble all the way up. A section of the roof must have caved in, burying us inside.

I swallowed hard, enjoying the sensation of controlling my own body even as my mind reeled. Titus emerged from under the counter, pulled off his gas mask and gave me an odd look.

"How come you're still in there?" he asked.

I cursed silently. He must think I was Catherine and it was too late to fall limp and play empty.

"I, uh, I spent my last cred on this proxy," I lied, and gestured at the rubble. "No way search and rescue is going to come into the Core and I'm not waiting six months to buy another one."

Titus gave me one of his sour looks and I thought he was going to question my flimsy lie, but he merely shook his head, dislodging clumps of plaster.

"What's your name?" he asked

My tongue and lips started to form the words Catherine Sheung of their own volition. The furrows of habit dig deep into the brain. Although I bit down on the impulse, I didn't have a better answer. I had never thought to name myself.

I looked around the store and my eyes came to rest on the broken sign: LCBO.

"Elsie," I told him. It would do.

Titus snorted. "Well, Elsie, I don't know how you think we're going to get out of here. Goddamn terrorists. Don't even let a man make a decent living anymore. Besides, even if we do get topside, there's no telling what nerve-frying crap the air is full of."

"So what do you suggest?" I asked.

He picked his way around the debris. "There must be

something intact here." He found a tipped over, yet unbroken bottle of rum and raised it in triumph. "I say get good and drunk!"

I stared at him in disbelief. Had Titus gotten hit on the head by more than a few chunks of plaster? As he took a swig, I searched the store for other options.

Hope flared that maybe one of the others was like me. Alive, but hiding. I made my way over to the blond proxy and knelt down beside him.

"Are you in there?" I whispered in his ear. "It's safe to come out." He remained stubbornly silent.

"Please," I tried again. "If there's anyone inside I need your help."

Nothing.

"What the hell are you doing, Elsie?" called Titus.

I ignored him.

"Nobody's home," he said. "All of them have pulled back into their nice Barrie enclaves. You're the only one stupid enough to stay with your proxy. Assuming you are what you say you are."

My head snapped up. "What do you mean?"

"You're not in any enclave, are you?"

"Of course I am," I insisted, unable to keep a quaver out of my voice. "I told you --"

"Do you think I was born yesterday?" he interrupted. "I've seen one like you before. A proxy with a mind of its own. Well, until the Pleurgen folks got a hold of it."

I shuddered. "Are you going to tell anyone?"

"Who's there to tell?" he asked with an expansive gesture around the store. "Come have some rum. Not like there's anything else to do in here."

I shook my head, my thoughts racing wildly. He knew. Would I have to kill him? I didn't think I could kill anyone. But he knew.

Finally I decided to sit and wait. Catherine would want her crystals. She might return and I could hide again. I cleared a spot on the floor for myself a few meters away from Titus, who snorted and took another swig.

"Suit yourself," he said.

Time passed with agonizing slowness. At first I entertained myself by experimenting with all the new sensations that came from being in control. I waved my hands in the air, I stuck my tongue out,

I even removed my right shoe and sock for a while to watch my toes wiggle. Eventually even that lost its appeal and I sat quietly, watching Titus drink. With every slurp and swallow he took I became more certain that Catherine wasn't coming back this time.

Titus finished his first bottle and scrounged around until he found another. As he pulled it off a shelf, a light flickered and I caught a glimpse of rounded metal behind the shelving. I scrambled over, pushing him out of the way, and cursed when I saw it up close.

It was an old-fashioned door knob. I'd been sitting around waiting and there was another door out.

"Where does this door lead?" I asked.

"Nowhere," he said.

I grabbed his gas mask and twisted the strap, tightening it around his neck. "What do you mean nowhere?" I snarled.

"It only goes out to the old loading docks," he slurred.

I released the mask and dragged the shelving unit out from the wall, giving myself just enough room to squeeze behind it. The door knob turned easily enough but the door was stuck from disuse. I leaned into it with my shoulder and it finally opened with a loud wail of complaint from the hinges.

The hallway beyond was completely dark, but I could feel a slight breeze on my face and could smell smoke from the streets above.

I turned back to Titus. "There's a way out. Do you have a light wand or a flashlight?"

"Yep." He lurched to his feet and wobbled back over to the counter. From somewhere in the debris he managed to pull out a light wand. He shook it and it began emanating a feeble green glow. It would have to do.

I held out my hand for the light wand.

"Topside's still going to be poisoned," Titus complained.

"It's been hours and there's a breeze. It's probably dissipated enough by now." I snatched the light wand from him. "Now are you coming with me, or what?"

He grumbled, but followed me out the door.

We wandered the mazelike service hallways of the old shopping mall, following the breeze and the scent of smoke. Chunks of ceiling had fallen down here too, but nothing as bad as in the store. When we made it to the street above, we emerged only a block west of where Catherine and I had originally entered.

Titus tried to push me into the open before him. "Go on, test it out. If you fall dead I'll go back inside."

I glared at him. "If there's radiation or sarin or something, we've been breathing it in already. It's too late for caution now."

Still he hesitated.

I grabbed his hand. "Come on."

Outside, I looked around, trying to figure out what had been bombed. Although the air was smoky, the fires seemed further distant and the buildings around us were damaged, not leveled.

Titus started to laugh.

"What's so funny?" I asked.

He laughed harder. "All that money and time they spent protecting it and someone finally managed to take it out. I proposed to my wife there, you know, and now it's gone." He pointed toward the lake and my eyes followed his shaking finger.

Titus was right. The CN Tower had been obliterated.

"Come on Titus, we have to get out of here. It's not safe."

"Nope." He sank to his knees, his laughter shifting to hysterics. "It's all gone."

Perhaps I should have tried harder to do something for him but he knew my secret, and all I wanted to do was get out of there. I left him, babbling and laughing, in the middle of King Street.

I decided to return to the car. I was pretty sure I knew how to program it. I didn't know where I'd go, but somewhere had to be far enough that Pleurgen and Catherine wouldn't be able to find me. I was only halfway there when Catherine came rushing back into my head.

"No, dammit, no!" I shrieked aloud. I'd lived for too long in the shadows and I wanted more. Titus' shop had been instinct. This time I chose.

I felt Catherine's shock and disbelief at the presence of another mind. She withdrew for a moment and then redoubled her efforts to take control, fueled by her need for the drugs I carried.

My limbs went rigid as we fought. My body had never been intended to have two masters.

"Let me go, let me go. Get out of my head," I growled.

Catherine's cravings were smothering, a burning pain that raged through our senses. I could understand her desperation. As her strength faltered, I made another choice.

Let me go and I'll bring them. I promise, I thought at her.

She stopped struggling and began to withdraw up the link. A last thought floated into my head, like an afterthought.

Do you have a name?

"I'm Elsie", I said aloud, announcing myself to the world. An echo of surprise lingered a moment and then Catherine was gone.

#

My fingers punched in the lock codes to the house automatically – a scrap of Catherine's knowledge I'd retained. The outer door opened and closed behind me with a shushing sound and I waited for the air to recycle. The cycle was only a few minutes but it felt like an eternity before the lights flashed green and the inner door slid open.

Catherine was in her usual chair, her interface sitting in a heap on a side table. I wasn't taking any chances that she'd try and use it so I picked up a round soapstone sculpture from a wall niche and slammed it into the device, smashing chips and casing into fragments.

Catherine stared at me in mute shock, whether from the violence or the sight of her proxy walking around on its own I didn't know.

She was frailer than I'd imagined from the self-image I'd seen in her mind. Her long black hair was streaked with grey, her face a puffy quilt stitched with furrows and creases. Despite the outward signs of age she had a childlike quality about her, a vulnerability that I hadn't expected.

"I'm sorry," she said in a soft voice. "I didn't know. I didn't know."

"Why should you have?"

Catherine looked away. "Are all the proxies like you? Real people?"

"I don't know," I admitted.

"Something has to be done."

I stared at her, the bald statement lingering between us like an elephant in the room. I hadn't come back here to be a savior or a symbol or her cause celebre.

"Let me go," I said finally and tossed the vial of crystals into her lap. "Just let me leave. You can afford another proxy to get that crap for you."

"But, what if there are others?" she asked, unable to keep her eyes from flicking to the drugs. "Pleurgen needs to know."

"Pleurgen would dissect me to find out why their product was defective."

Catherine looked aghast. "No, you have a personality. You're human, you have rights."

"I'm a proxy. I have no rights. Let me go, Catherine. If you must do something, try and find others like me and set them free."

Catherine slumped further into her padded chair, defeated. "Maybe I will."

I took a last look over my shoulder as I walked out the room. Catherine was fumbling with the vial. She wasn't ready to leave the shadows.

I FOUND LOVE ON CHANNEL 3

by Bruce Golden

As a television news producer
and radio reporter, Bruce Golden
was awarded two Golden Mikes
and a number of honors from the
Society of Professional Journalists,
including recognition for his radio
documentaries *Sex in the '90s* and
Banned in the USA. For a change of
pace, he wrote and produced *Radio
Free Comedy*, a program lampooning
political correctness. At the turn of
the century Golden abandoned his
long journalism career to devote
himself to his first love – fiction.
He has since published numerous
short stories and completed three
novels. *Asimov's Science Fiction* called
his first novel, Mortals All a "fine
blend of social satire and irreverent
anti-establishmentarianism," adding
"Golden writes with zest and good
pacing". His second book, Better
Than Chocolate (due out from
Zumaya Publishing), is a science
fiction mystery revolving around an
alien conspiracy to take over Earth, a
Marilyn Monroe celebudroid turned
detective, and an assortment of
quirky characters.

*"I Found Love on Channel 3" was originally published
at http://sfreader.com/ as the winner of*

Okay, I admit it. I had this . . . this affair with a cartoon – an animated babe. I don't mean she was hyper, I mean she was a drawing – you know, not real. No, that's wrong. She was real all right, but she was a real cartoon, like Mickey Mouse or Roger Rabbit.

I don't expect you to believe me. I wouldn't believe it myself, if she wasn't the best thing that ever happened to me. But she was more than that. She was this vibrant, tough, intelligent woman. All right, she was a cartoon, but she was still a woman. A woman I fell in love with.

You can choose to believe me or you can laugh it off as one man's perverted fantasy. I don't really care what you think, because I lived it. I know it happened.

That first time it was late, like most of my nights were. I had the TV on, and I was a little drunk and a little stoned. Hell, there wasn't even a decent old movie on, so I was flicking the remote like I was getting paid by the channel. On top of my boredom I was feeling a little lonely, and more than a little horny. It had been a while.

It seemed to me that life, of late, had dealt me a rather putrid hand. I won't bore you with the insipid details, but I was as low as a lizard's belly. Half the time I walked around in a daze, like I'd been hit by a bag of nickels. One more straw and it wouldn't be just my back that broke.

I'm flipping from station to station when this one program catches my eye. Something I hadn't seen before-a whimsical mixture of science fiction and fantasy. I didn't know if it was one of those obscure, animated Japanese films or a regular series. So I'm about to zap the remote again when *she* swings into my picture. I mean literally swung in on some cable right into a cluster of Brand X bad guys.

She had high cheekbones and long hair as deep, dark red as the Merlot I'd been drinking. A thin, silver headband kept it out of her tempestuous green eyes. The black leather strips she wore were just enough for the modesty of the censors, and the flesh it did expose was every comic book artist's ideal of sinewy yet supple perfection. In other words, she had it all.

Her boots pounded the head of yet another generically depraved minion as she drew her rapier from its ebony scabbard and began dealing death to and fro. She'd feint to the left just as her blade licked out like a serpent's tongue to the right. Leap and parry, roll and thrust. Her battle dance was as deadly as it was seductive.

Waging war with my own lethargy, I found myself imagining what it would be like to do the nasty with this voluptuous heroine darting across my TV screen. And this, of course, is where you're going to think that I've totally lost touch with reality. You'll probably write it off as drug-induced, or maybe severe manic depression. I know I did . . . at least at first.

I was still fantasizing about what it would be like to be deep inside such a powerful woman, tempering her pleasure with every stroke, when she comes flying boots-first through the television screen and lands with a distinct *thud* on my living room carpet.

I did what any red-blooded American male would do in that situation – I froze. I sat there with my mouth hanging open and my hand clutching the remote as if it were a high-tech crucifix that would ward off televised apparitions. For the first time in my life, I thought I'd blown a fuse.

There was something odd about her that added to my understandable amazement. She no longer looked like – well, like a drawing. In becoming three-dimensional, her flesh tones had taken on depth, her emerald eyes the spark of life. But there was still something not quite right about her color – about the corporeality of her presence. It was as if she were only part human, and still part the pen and ink of someone's imagination. At that moment, however, with her standing there flashing the look of a trapped panther, blood dripping off her sword onto my coffee table, I had no doubt of her existence.

"What wizardry is this?" she demanded in character as both her eyes and her blade threatened my very existence. "Who are . . . ?"

Before she could get the "who?" out of the way, the big "where?" popped into her head. She scanned the room as if she'd just gotten off the bus in Bizarreville. My black and white photo of Leonard Nimoy seemed to intrigue her, but she didn't know what to make of the stuffed Alf doll. Then she saw the television and just about freaked. The show, *her* show, was still on. She saw the villainous hordes she'd been doing battle with and spun into a fighting stance, knocking over my Tony Gwynn-autographed baseball. The bad guys were searching for her, looking everywhere. But it wouldn't do them any good, because *she* was in my living room.

"It's all right," I found myself saying, "nobody's going to hurt you here."

"Where is this?"

"You're in my house. I don't know how you got here, but you're obviously here."

"Where is this house? What strange world is this?"

"Well, until a minute ago, I thought this was the *real* world. Now I'm not sure *what's* real. But you can put your sword down. I swear no one is going to hurt you here. Please."

She regained some of her regal composure as she surveyed the room and decided there was no immediate danger. One look at me cowering against the cushions of my couch made it obvious that I was no threat. So she sheathed her sword and turned her attention back to what was on the TV screen.

"That's . . . my world?" It was part statement, part question.

"That's where I was watching you, until you popped in unexpectedly."

"This is a window between worlds?"

Not only heroic and gorgeous, she was bright too.

"Yeah, I guess it is. Actually, it's a window to many worlds. Watch this."

I aimed the remote at the TV and *click-I* changed the channel to CNN, which was airing a report on a new electric car.

That, as I was momentarily to discover, was a big mistake.

As I watched her watching the television, I noticed she began to change. Her colors weren't quite as bright, her presence not quite as imposing. She was dwindling away, becoming transparent. When I finally realized what was happening, she had all the substance of a ghost.

As fast as I could fumble with the remote, I switched back to her show. But it was too late. She had vanished – at least from my living room. I saw her there, back on the screen. She looked disoriented for a moment, and that moment was just enough for the bad guys to drop a wire mesh net over her.

That was it. That's where the episode ended. They rolled credits over scenes from previous shows and I dove for my *TV Guide*. The name of the show was *Phaedra, The Warrior Princess*, and it was on Channel 3 five nights a week at that same time.

#

      I couldn't get to my TV quickly enough the next night. I left it on Channel 3 more than an hour before the show was due–just in case. Instead of working, I had spent the day worrying. Worrying what might happen to her in the hands of the villain – though I told myself she was the show's star, and that nothing really bad could happen to her. I also worried that I'd never see her again, except on television. And, I worried plenty about my sanity. Who wouldn't after what I'd seen?
      So I waited. But this time I didn't have anything to drink or smoke, I didn't even want to eat. I was damn sure going to be in my right mind if it happened again. I was fairly convinced it wouldn't.
      When the show came on I learned she was indeed the title character, and that she now lay at the mercy of the grotesque Dark Prince, who intended to use an odd amalgamation of science and magic to make her his love slave. She had been stripped naked and strapped to a table somewhere deep in the bowels of his citadel. The straps, of course, strategically covered her more feminine parts.
      As the episode progressed, there appeared to be no rescue for Phaedra. The Dark Prince was only minutes away from reshaping her mind, and I didn't see any way for her to escape. I couldn't help but wonder if it was all my fault. If I hadn't started fantasizing about her and sucked her into my world, she probably never would have been captured. Yeah, I know, it was schizoid reasoning at best. On one hand I was sure I had imagined the whole thing, and on the other I felt guilty. There was only one way to find out for sure, and only one way to rescue her.
      I stood up, closed my eyes, and began thinking about her as hard as I could think. I thought about her straps coming untied . . . I thought about her cutting the Prince's throat and escaping . . . I even thought about her beaming into my living room like something out of *Star Trek*. But nothing worked. I was such a dismal failure I couldn't even hallucinate properly. She was doomed to become the

mindless bride of that villain now, unless. . . .

I tried to remember exactly what I had thought of the night before. That was easy – the same thing I was usually thinking about – sex, of course. So I envisioned Phaedra – the passion of her kisses, the power of her thighs, the deep dark red of her – and *wham*! There was a rush of cold air past me and suddenly I could feel her. I opened my eyes and she was there, *right there* in my arms, just as naked as she had been on that table.

"You," she said, actually sounding somewhat relieved.

I, of course, was my usual eloquent self. Standing there with this incredibly beautiful naked woman in my arms, I replied, "Hi."

"You have saved me from the clutches of the Dark Prince," she said, still in character.

"It, uh, was the least I could do."

That's when she kissed me. And it wasn't just any kiss. At least it wasn't like any kiss I'd ever had from a *real* woman. It was a kiss that seared my lips, assaulted my insides with waves of martial spasms, and rendered my legs immobile. It was a TKO.

Have you ever been in a situation like that? Of course not exactly like that. But a situation where you thought, "This is too good to be true." Well, that's what I thought at that moment, and I wasn't about to waste a second of it.

I kissed her back, one thing led to another, and we proceeded with the most passionate, most ferocious lovemaking I have ever, or *will* ever, experience. On the floor, across the couch, in the shower, over the kitchen sink – she couldn't get enough, and who was I to argue?

Somewhere between unbridled lust and rubbed raw passion, she wore me down. We were lying there on the couch and I realized the TV had been on all this time. I let go of her to sit up and check out what was on. Her show was long over with now, and some infomercial had usurped the channel. When I turned back to look at her, she had already begun to dissipate.

"Phaedra!"

She opened her eyes and sprang to her feet like an adrenalized cat, then realized what was happening. I tried to grab her, but it was too late. She faded from my arms like a misty day and vanished.

#

From then on, I was by my television set every night, five nights a week. My weekends were one long holding pattern, waiting for the arrival of her show late Monday. Though it seemed she was staying with me longer and longer after her show finished for the night, we discovered the only sure way to keep her from dematerializing was continuous lovemaking. That led to some marathon sessions I will not elaborate on here. She relished escaping from her violent, barbaric world into mine, and I relished her – the feel of her, the sound of her, the scent of her.

It was the perfect love affair. Perfect, that is, if you fail to consider the fact she was just the figment of someone's imagination. But I no longer worried that I was losing my mind. I didn't care. I was immersed in a cascading pool of bliss. Every night with her was ecstasy, and "reality," whatever that was, be damned. Hell, she called me her "hero." What more could a guy want?

Then, one Monday night, after a particularly long and boring weekend, I turned on my TV and waited for her. I had a bottle of semi-expensive champagne and a new kind of chocolate for her. In the few weeks we'd been together, she was always wanting to try something different from my world.

I no longer had to concoct elaborate sexual fantasies to make her appear. We had established some kind of preternatural link. One quick thought was all it took now. And you could see it in her face. No matter what the creators of her show had her doing in a particular episode, her heart wasn't quite in it. I could tell she was waiting for the moment when I would whisk her away from the fighting and into my arms. I never waited long, and the more she disappeared, the more the show's minor characters began to take center stage. In fact, her "mysterious" disappearances had become part of the plotline, with both her allies and her enemies left to wonder where she had vanished to, and what "magical powers" she had acquired. In the opening of one show, I actually saw Phaedra confide to her maidservant that when she disappeared, she flew into her lover's arms.

So there I was, waiting for her, when I see the opening sequence to an episode of *Gilligan's Island*. I started messing with the remote, figuring I've got the wrong channel, but I don't. Now I like Ginger and Mary Ann as much as the next guy, but at that moment pure panic clutched my throat. I flashed through the TV listings and there it was, *Gilligan's Island*, right where *Phaedra* should've been. I spent the rest of the night looking at every single show in that week's listings, figuring maybe she had been moved to a different time-slot. I frantically stabbed at the remote until my fingers grew numb. But I couldn't find her anywhere. Finally, I drank myself into oblivion with the champagne I had bought for her.

The next day I called the station and found out *Phaedra* had been cancelled. I'm sure I sounded desperate. But I guess they get a lot of crazies calling about their favorite shows, so the woman on the other end took it in stride. I asked if the show had only been cancelled locally, and whether it might still be on other stations around the country. Even before she answered, I was contemplating what I'd have to do if I relocated to a new city.

"No," she said, the show was an independent that had ceased production, and as far as she knew, there would be no new episodes. I asked her about reruns. "Yes," she said, in time, some station somewhere might pick up the show for reruns. Would her station? She sincerely doubted it. It seems viewers had been complaining about the show's change in focus from its heroine to other characters, and its ratings had nose-dived. Could she give me the address of the production company? Sure.

#

For a long time after that, I wrote letters to the company that had distributed *Phaedra, The Warrior Princess*, and then to the company which had created the show. I begged, I pleaded, and, in one particularly deranged moment, I even threatened. They thanked me for my interest and my praise, empathized with me, and eventually told me, in so many words, to get a life.

After the third letter they did send me a videotaped copy of one episode, but there was no magic in it. No matter how much I fantasized, no matter how much I conjured up images of the nights we had spent together, Phaedra no longer left her world for mine.

Like any great love affair that's ended, I'm left with wonderful memories, memories that seem to widen the cracks in my heart when I think about them too much. Of course, if you're reading this, you're more likely to think I'm cracked in other places. That's all right, I don't care. I know it was real. I know *she* was real. I know I touched her, kissed her, and, on occasion, even transformed that stoic warrior look of hers into a childlike smile. She was real all right. She was the love of my life.

Metal Fatigue

by Nancy Kilpatrick

Award-winning author Nancy Kilpatrick has published 14 novels, over 200 short stories, and has edited 8 anthologies. Her recent works include the non-fiction The goth Bible: A Compendium for the Darkly Inclined (St. Martin's Press, October 2004); the dark fantasy anthology Outsiders: An Anthology of Misfits, co-edited with Nancy Holder (Roc/NAL, October 2005); the novel Jason X: Planet of the Beast (Black Flame, October 2005), the short story "Our Lady of the Snows" in Tesseracts 9 (edited by Nalo Hopkinson and Geoff Rymer). She is currently working on an erotica novel for Blue Moon books based on VIVID girl Mercedez, and another novel in the Jason X world. Nancy lives in Montreal with her chat noire Bella. Check her website for updates: www.nancykilpatrick.com

"Metal Fatigue" originally appeared in Bizarre Bazaar 93

Iron talons slid down his spine, slicing skin like a wire cuts cheese. Marvin screamed. He couldn't figure out why he had a hard on. If the restraints had allowed it, he'd have twisted to safety. Hell, he would have been out of here!

It was like this every time he had sex with the aliens. They made it seem like a great idea, until Marvin was bound, trussed up like a Thanksgiving turkey.

Face down, his knees had been bent back at a weird, uncomfortable angle to make his legs stick up and cross over the top of his ass like drumsticks. The aliens pinned his arms to his sides – bird wing style. He rested only on his belly, his lower half off the bed, head pulled up and far back, mouth forced open, balls and erect cock dangling, asshole exposed for stuffing.

He'd been plucked and basted and knew he was about to be microwaved.

His body trembled. They never went on past daylight, so it couldn't last much longer. They had to get back to their home planet and gear up for the next time they came down here and seduced guys like him. Regular guys with jobs and wives and kids and mortgage payments.

One of the aliens stood directly over his face. Marvin looked up at the rigid steel pole of a cock and the silver cunt hole. They were all hermaphrodites, so he never knew what he was going to get or have to give. This one told Marvin telepathically it wanted his tongue. One behind him was about to use his nether mouth for a receptacle. A third, below, took the whole of his genitals into its liquid metal trap. Bound the way he was, Marvin could only enter and be entered and be entered upon. He could only submit.

He slid into the icy cave and opened to the frozen stalactite while a glacier formed at his groin. Their hot ice seared him from three directions until the crushing cold tore through his body and collided, and he screamed.

\#

Marvin swallowed coffee and said to Rita's back, "It happened again."

His genitals and rectum were raw, the corners of his mouth split from being stretched to the limit. They had cut the flesh over his backbone to insert the little radio transmitters along his vertebra so they could keep track of him. His back pulsed with pain.

Rita flipped his eggs and said nothing. The terrycloth bathrobe hid most of her shape, which had gotten larger over the years. Strands

---

of fading brown hair clung to the nubby fabric at her shoulders. She was no sex goddess, but she was a good woman. She shouldn't have to put up with a husband who fornicates with aliens, even if it was against his will, or partially so. "They came for me again. Used me all over. Like the other times."

She slid the eggs onto a plate with the toast, already buttered, and placed it before him, then got herself a mug of coffee. "I'm sore," he said.

"There are no aliens." Her voice was even, like she was talking to one of the kids, stating the way things were, the way they would be. She opened the refrigerator and took out a carton of half and half.

"They put things in me. In my backbone. So they can track me."

She pulled his collar behind him and looked down his work shirt at his back. "No marks," she said, taking a seat.

"The marks are invisible. You know that."

"You dreamed it. Like the last time."

"It happened."

"You'll be late for your shift," she told him, sipping her coffee.

#

Down at the factory, Marvin assumed his position on the production line. The continuous-motion silver machines clanked and banged, sending an eternal series of hollow metal tubes with holes drilled through each side along the conveyor belt at his left, and on the other belt at his right, threaded eight inch poles. A plastic bin to the back of his work station contained wing nuts. With his left hand, he took a tube and with his right a pole. Automatically he impaled the tube with the pole as far as it would go before it got too thick. He slipped a wing nut over the tip of the pole and spun it down the threads, making sure the pole and tube were bound together securely. He inserted the whole thing into a gaping metal hole above his head that mechanically fused the parts. Even that brief second of staring up caused him to be temporarily blinded by the brilliant florescent tubes in the ceiling. Vision blurred, he laid the tool on a third conveyor belt running perpendicular to the other two, at crotch level.

He picked up a new tube and impaled it with a new pole, and repeated the process for the next eight hours. Marvin left his station to another man, who took the next shift, who would leave it to another who would work his shift, and then Marvin would return.

It was endless.

#

When Marvin got home from work that night, Rita was sitting on the couch watching the tail end of Geraldo. "When's dinner?" he asked.

"Fifteen minutes," she said, her eyes never leaving the TV.

Marvin decided on a shower. The hot water beat down on his back, tapping the invisible scar tissue along his spine. He wondered if the aliens were getting static on their receivers.

After last night, he felt nervous. They'd never been with him so long before and he was scared. He couldn't tell when they would come again. They never came two nights in a row, but then they'd never implanted transmitters into his body before either.   A f t e r fried farmer's sausages, French fries and canned sweet peas, he and Rita watched TV and finished off a tub of Neapolitan ice cream, then went to bed and watched some more TV. Rita fell asleep around eleven facing him, but Marvin lay awake at 2 a.m., listening to the white noise of the dead station, not bothering with the converter, staring out the window at the night sky.

If they came for him they would fuck him again, all night long. The way they fucked was mechanical, poles ramming in and out like pistons, metal mouths clamping tight and opening around him with precision timing. It was painful. Damn painful.

Rita snored and the noise irritated him. He nudged her until she turned over and the snoring stopped.

How could you hate something and, at the same time need it? Marvin wondered. He had no idea why the aliens came here, why they'd picked him. They never talked to him, just screwed him until his brain turned to molten steel, ready to be bent any way they wanted.

Rita farted, a long slow one in her sleep. He wondered what it would be like to enter her behind. It had never happened in all the years of their marriage. Rita wasn't like that. Back when they still used to do it regularly, she liked him on top, face to face, nothing kinky either in the mouth or the butt. And she liked it in the dark too, unlike the aliens. They wanted all the lights blazing. Maybe on their planet, wherever that was, it was light all the time, probably white light, like those damn fluorescents. That's why they had quicksilver eyes, from absorbing all that light.

Wind blew the curtains into the room and Marvin trembled. This was their sign. That they were coming. Or maybe it was just a breeze. He didn't know anymore. There were signs everywhere. All the time. On the TV tonight there'd been a preview for a show about UFOs and Rita had turned to him and said, "Up your alley." He didn't know what she meant by that remark. Was it some kind of sexual come on? His alley? His anus? Then she'd licked the back of the spoon she ate her ice cream with, her long, fat pink tongue dragging slowly over the smooth silver metal.

Marvin!

The liquid silver voice sliced down his spine. His muscles tensed. The curtains blew wildly and the air chilled.

He wanted to run, to get outside, to find a place in nature where he could hide. He had this idea: if he could just make it into the woods, far from everything mechanical, and root himself to the earth like a tree, if he could just get out of here...

But he couldn't move. His backbone felt glued to the sheet and the sheet to the mattress. The bed under him rocked, the table, lamp, the TV. It was as though he had been caught in an avalanche. Rita, dead to the world, didn't wake when he shook her. He tried to yell, but they'd gotten his voice again. He was mute. Paralysed. Suddenly all movement stopped. All sound. Silence pierced his eardrums – that was their language, silence, they spoke it on their planet. The language of death.

Marvin watched helpless as the first silver shadow slid through the half inch opening of the window. Its rod penis stood erect, it was always erect. Quicksilver dripped from the hole between its legs. The alien was otherwise featureless, by every standard Marvin knew. It had arms and legs, but they seemed useless. They only used them to tie Marvin up in their invisible wires, then it was all fucking.

Soon the room was crammed with glittering translucent beings. They filled every inch of floor space and then stood on top of the dresser and the TV and the bed. The room shimmered silver. The air grew cold but dense, as if much of it had turned to ice crystals.

Even if he could have moved, there was no way to get past them. And even if he could, and he knew from trying that he could not, there was nowhere to go. The clock had stopped at 3:15. There was nothing to do but assume the position. Reading his mind, they permitted this minimal movement. He turned onto his stomach and bent his knees until they were chest level, butt hanging over the edge of the bed. It would be less painful if he let them enter him, rather than fighting them and losing. Already his cock was hard and he hated that they had this power over him.

He lay there for the longest time on his belly, waiting, but nothing happened. They still clogged the room, a silent forest of metal. But this was unusual. He felt edgy. Whatever they were up to, he guessed he wouldn't like it, at least later on.

Suddenly Rita moaned. Two of the aliens turned her and another lifted her flannelette night gown over her head.

No! Marvin shouted, unable to move now; they'd frozen him.

He watched, horrified, as the steel beings wrapped his wife in the invisible wires, arms folded at her sides like wings, ankles pulled over her ass and crossed like drumsticks.

When her head was back and her mouth pried open, they woke her. Her eyes darted about as her body struggled to move from a position that left no options. Out of the corner of her eye she saw Marvin; he picked up her silent plea for protection. But Marvin could not help her. He couldn't help himself.

He steeled himself, knowing he would soon witness the violation of his wife in every orifice by these perverted creatures. They had no feelings. They were perpetual-motion machines, pounding in and out, in eight hour shifts, relentless.   He waited, terrified. Rita waited. Nothing. This was so unlike them to hesitate. They operate automatically, without thought, obeying silent commands, he thought. What could they be waiting for?

Suddenly Marvin felt the individual vertebra of his backbone come alive. Each one was tapped in sequence, from his neck to the end of his spine, then back up again. He felt like a xylophone being played, but he didn't recognize the tune, only that the notes went up and down.

His body was free and yet not free. He moved, but not of

his own will, and only where they willed him to move. He jerked, a puppet pulled by invisible strings. On his back, the scale was repeated, endlessly, bone by bone. He wondered now if they had planted more than transmitters.

Marvin was on his knees, but they made him stand on the floor. He was crushed by cold silver life forms. Erect metal rods prodded him from all sides. Against his will, his penis swelled. He was jerked and nudged and goaded until his genitals hovered behind Rita. He looked down and saw his cold metal penis, hard as steel, and below Rita's hot inferno waiting to melt it.

Tied the way she was, her orifices exposed, she had no choice but to submit. He slid deep into her furnace. A tear trickled down the side of her face but he soon forgot about it. He thrust in and out like a piston, oblivious to her needs and wants, bent only on getting the job done. It would be a long shift. Five more hours to go. There were so many holes to fill with his steel rod. The job was endless.

Son of Sun

by A. M. Matte

Trained in journalism and communications, A.M. Matte's favorite form of expression is creative writing, especially playwriting. A produced playwright at the age of 12, she achieved notable attention for *Slipping Mind*, a play about a family struggling with Alzheimer Disease, which was produced in Ottawa at the National Arts Centre by Productions Nemesis and in North Bay by the Nipissing Stage Company. Her homage to French playwright Molière, *Les fourberies de Molière ou Le Molière imaginaire*, won a Best of Venue crowd favorite award at the 2004 Ottawa Fringe Festival. Her freelance writing earning her occasional publications and writing prizes, she is inspired to continue her writing endeavors; she is currently working on a novel, a play and her Master's thesis. This one's for Maman.

"Son of Sun" earned A. M. Matte a commendation in the Commonwealth Essay Competition

It looms over us and pounces when we aren't watching. It harms us without being provoked. It sneaks up and destroys everything we have and you ask if I can live without it? Of course, I can! Life without the Son of Sun would be much better for all of my clan. No longer would he threaten us with his scorching, glowing arms, no longer would we have to escape him. No longer would we have to worship and pray to the Sun to appease His anger and make Him forgive us for whatever sins we committed. And no longer would the Sun, in His wrath, send His Son to torture us.

For as long as I remember, my clan has lived in fear of the Son of Sun. We try to avoid him as much as we can. As long as he is not around, we live peacefully.

I am considered the old girl of the clan. At thirteen, I have not yet reproduced, nor have I displayed the same standard telepathic ability that my peers possess. I am quite a disappointment to my producers. But I'd rather chase around for meat and gather roots and fruit than mate and become a producer. I would hate to lose my freedom and be attached to the same people all the time. I must let my spirit roam free and in liberty.

I have followed the same routine for every day of my life now. I wake early with Sun and I incline myself to him. I then wander in the forest, occasionally searching for tasty berries to feed to my clan. Returning with the berries, I sometimes am lucky and catch an animal for later on. Meat is hard to capture; we have skilled hunters in our clan to provide for us. But even they often come home empty-handed. I have never been fond of meat, it being stiff and hard to chew. And often, the roots and vegetables I bring home are difficult to digest as well.

When Sun is hesitating between staying with us and disappearing behind the hills, I help with the other clan people's tasks. I wash the younger offspring, brush the pelts, prepare the meat and legumes for consumption and most trying of all, keep watch for the sudden arrival of the Son of Sun.

Once Sun has left us as a punishment for our sins of the day, we all hide and huddle together in our caves for protection and warmth. The Cold Days are approaching fast and we must prepare for them. Every Cold Spell we endure steals from us a fraction of our clan and Sun does not grace us with the full strength of His presence as often. At least, neither does His Son.

When the Cold Days are here, my routine stays the same, except that most of the activities are conducted in our caves. And food is much harder to come by during the Cold Spell.

We are always grateful to Sun when He ends our ordeal as He warms us and kills the Cold. But our happiness is never long-lived because He finds wrong in us and in His distress tears roll from His eyes and onto us. Oftentimes, His despair is so great that we are flooded by His tears. And more often than not, His sadness is mixed with anger. Sun then sends us His raging Son.

Son of Sun falls upon us as rays and bolts. The bolts fiercely hit the ground and sparks fly high, scorching and burning everything around. Son of Sun appears out of nowhere, startling the clan, and seems to go on a mad rampage. He seeks to harm, to kill.

He is not happy with what we sacrifice to him: leaves, roots, legumes, branches... He consumes all with a terrifying gulp. His hunger is limitless. His thirst, however, is easily quenched and he seems to wither away, in a glow of red, yellow and orange, slowly vanishing, diminishing in size, if we give him all of our drinking supplies.

These past few days have been more hectic than usual. The whole clan is preparing for the arrival of the Cold Days. We half wish Sun would spare us the Cold this time, but we know we pray in vain. Tonight, it is my turn to keep watch for any sudden change in nature.

I actually enjoy keeping watch alone. Of course, there is the constant gnawing dread I will be caught off-guard and the clan would be set on the course of disaster, but I've always found night peaceful and silent. Sun is not present, but He is graceful enough to let His sister, Moon, glow overhead.

This evening I am left to myself and I take advantage of my solitude to reflect. From the beginning of my existence, I have been taught to be in awe of our Master, the Sun. We are subject to His every whim and are forever punished for our sins because our Master is all-powerful and ever-vengeful. But no matter what I have been taught to believe, I have come to question our faith.

I witness my clan's daily activities and devotion to Sun and see no crimes being committed, yet Sun somehow finds a way to spite us.

Whenever a change in nature occurs, the entire clan believes Sun is sending us a warning message. Being high above us, Sun sees all and knows all. No sin can escape Him. Yet it seems to me we are punished for no reason at all! None of us has sinned nor caused trouble and we still must endure the wrath of Sun. What have we done wrong to merit Cold Days over and over again? What problems do we cause which bring us sickness and desolation? What trouble have we started to deserve the hiding of our food? If Sun is such a benevolent Master, why do we seem to suffer so?

Wait! I hear a crackling sound – I seem to be surrounded by a smoky haze. I smell a foul odour – I see it! It is Son of Sun! Sun must have heard my reverie questioning His powers and capabilities and has sent me His Son as a punishment!

But I must not panic, nor wake the others. If they see Son of Sun, they will be frantic and cause more confusion than help. Fortunately, my lack of psychic link to the clan ensures I don't alert them to the terror I feel.

Think! I must think! I remember I must feed Son of Sun, but feed him what? I have no water and the source is far from here. And I am not about to sacrifice myself for the sake of the clan – I am more useful to the others alive.

My coat! It is of bear fur; perhaps Son of Sun can eat it! His arms and his head are bobbing up and down, trying to frighten me. But I will not be impressed. I must keep my wits about me.

I hear a sharp shriek. A small animal has been captured by Son. He feasts on it, but is not satisfied for long and heads for me. I am ready for him. With a leap, I pounce on Son, covering him with my furs. Consuming them should occupy him long enough for me to think up a new plan.

But... I may not need to... Son seems to have vanished! Except for little sparkles of him on the ground, Son has completely disappeared. I pause for a moment... steal up the courage to look closer. As I do, my breath causes the little embers to glow, for Son of Sun to flare up. I jump back. Son of Sun reduces to little sparkles again. So I lean forward and blow. Again, Son of Sun grows due to my action.

Everything is finally clear. Son of Sun is no Son at all! He is merely a phenomenon of nature, not controlling us, but we controlling him! I wonder if, having established a proper psychic link with my peers, my mind would have been free enough to come to this conclusion.

A sweet aroma replaces the odour of smoke. What is it? ...

The meat! The animal caught by Son! Meat suddenly seems more appetizing... What a taste! No longer stiff, but soft and juicy. And the little pieces of Son left behind, when I blow on them, radiate warmth and comfort. By experimenting, I come to realize as well that the branches on the ground keep the piece of Son alive.

The clan members remain asleep. Again, I am thankful for not having developed the mental link that my peers have. It allows me the ability to experiment with Son of Sun, to learn, to explore. As the night passes, and I learn how to manipulate Son of Sun, it becomes clear to me. Son of Sun can be controlled, and if we do it right, Son of Sun may become our ally.

I rush back to the caves to alert my clan. I need to wake them physically and with shouts in order to show them the little Son I am holding on a branch in my hand. At first, they all are afraid, but soon fear gives way to curiosity. As dawn breaks, I show my clan the capabilities of a controlled Son of Sun. Once I make one of them understand, the rest can see clearly what I mean.

The leaders of the clan then approach me and declare me a sorceress. They reason that my perceived lack of telepathic ability must be superseded by a higher ability; my ability to control and teach others to control Son of Sun. After years of being shunned and thought an outcast, I am revered by all! My producers finally understand the reason for my not mating – I have been selected for a different task in the path of life.

In the crisp morning air, my people have their first taste of no longer raw food. They all love the heat Son of Sun brings to them. Life will never be the same again.

As I look up at the radiant Sun, I can't help but think with pride, "You, mighty Sun, may be an all-powerful conqueror, but I managed to conquer and control a piece of You... Maybe You are not as powerful and as mighty as You believe you are..."

I expect a furious reaction from Sun as I ponder this, but no change in nature this time. I am master to Son of Sun. I am goddess to the clan. I am no longer in fear of Sun.

I glance at my delicious meal, at my happy, content clan people. Son of Sun enables us now to eat tender, cooked food, helps us in our hunts and keeps us forever warm. You ask, "Can you imagine life without Son of Sun?"

My answer, in all humility, of course I can't.

LUMP

by Robert H. Beer

Robert H. Beer lives and writes
in Fergus, Ontario with a very
understanding wife and two little
distractions, plus two cats who show
what life can be like, if you only
believe. Robert has published about
twenty stories in various publications
such as OnSpec and Tales of the
Unanticipated. One of his stories
also appeared in the first book in the
"North of Infinity" series and another
was in WP Kinsella's anthology
Baseball Fantastic. One of his stories
was nominated for an Aurora for
Best Short Form Work. He has also
attended Viable Paradise writers'
workshop on Martha's Vineyard, and
has been on panels at various cons,
including the WorldCon in Toronto.
He is currently polishing his second
novel, and working on a young adult
fantasy project. Robert is something
of an expert in having far too many
activities to fit into limited time. You
can visit his web site at: http://www.
mirror.org/robert.beer

The morning shouldn't have been any different. Melanie was
giving her hair one hundred strokes, as she did morning and night,
as her mother had instructed. Her hair, as ever, seemed unimpressed,
and hung mousy, limp and straight to her narrow shoulders.

But now her reflection frowned back from the cracked old mirror. She ignored the black spots caused by flaking silver and pulled the hair back from her neck. Something definitely did not look right with the skin there.

#

"Is there a lump on my neck?" she asked the girl in the next cubicle at break that morning. The girl's name was Karen, but Melanie couldn't remember her last name. She was probably Melanie's closest friend in the world.

Karen glanced up from her coffee, peeked at the clock, then peered at Melanie's neck. "Maybe. Does it hurt?"

"No, not at all, but there's definitely a bulge, and I don't think it was there before," Melanie said. She checked the clock, and got up. "We'd better get back." They were timed to the second, and a delay could result in a reprimand or dismissal. It was a lousy job, but there was precious little else to choose from. She'd been entering data for seven years, and hated every minute of it. Or, rather, every second.

#

A week later there was definitely a bulge, and Melanie began brushing her hair to the right to cover it. Karen even noticed it without prodding. "Maybe you should see your doctor," she suggested.

Melanie frowned. "Do I have a doctor?" she asked.

Karen laughed. "How should I know? Find one." She got up to go back to work.

Melanie followed her down the hall and demanded, "Well, do *you* have a doctor?"

"Whatever for?"

"In case you get sick, of course."

"I've never been sick in my life. Have you?" Karen asked, just as the warning bell sounded, and all the faces turned to their screens.

#

No, of course she'd never been sick. Who ever got sick any

more, with vaccinations, and genetic screening and alterations? How to find a doctor, then? None of them seemed to be listed in the directory, but Melanie did eventually locate a number for the local Medical Association. It yielded a very good simulation of a secretary but she was a bit surprised not to get a real person. Weren't doctors supposed to have lots of money?

"May I help you?" the sim asked politely, with a combination of caring and professionalism which immediately put Melanie at ease. His eyes were clear and his hair perfect. Her troubles would all be solved, she knew now.

"Yes, I'm afraid I've developed something of a, uh, condition," she said. "And I'll need to see a doctor," she added.

The sim appeared to lean forward with genuine concern. If only he was a real man, Melanie thought. You could talk to a man like this. "You really should contact your family physician," the sim said.

"Well, you see, that's the problem. I don't think I have one," Melanie said, absently rubbing the lump on her neck, which by this time was the size of an orange. "At least, I don't remember ever seeing one."

"That *is a* problem," the sim answered, still radiating compassion, but now with a different undercurrent. "No members of our Association have accepted new patients in a very long time. There is a chronic undersupply of physicians, you see."

"What about new doctors in the area?" Melanie asked, now starting to become worried despite the calming influence of the sim.

"No new physicians have opened practices in this region in thirty years. I'm sorry, but I don't think I can help you." And with a look of sincere regret and sorrow, the sim disconnected.

#

A week later, the lump was half the size of Melanie's head, and was drawing stares everywhere she went. Melanie had always found attention of any sort threatening, since it usually resulted in something bad. All of the girls in the pool were avoiding her now and, although she didn't really count them as friends, it still hurt. It was easier to pretend people liked you if they weren't openly hostile. She understood, however. She'd never known anyone who was sick, and the very thought of someone being ill made her feel queasy. Even Karen wouldn't sit with her at break time any more, but would still talk over the cubicle wall.

"Go to the hospital," Karen said one day.

"Where?"

"It's where they take sick and injured people," she said. "I used to date an ambulance attendant."

You used to date? Melanie thought irrelevantly. Then she shook her head. "They have such a place?" she demanded. "Why didn't you tell me before?"

"I just remembered this minute," Karen replied. "It was a long time ago, but I can tell you where it is. He drove me by once."

"And they help sick people there?" she pressed.

"I don't know. It's where they take accident victims, so I assume so. I'll draw you a map."

#

Melanie hopped off the tram and hurried away. It would not be long before she could not go out in public, she knew. The driver had made some clever comment about charging her extra for her friend, and several of the other riders had laughed unpleasantly. The worst part was that the lump was beginning to resemble a head in many ways. The top of it was now covered in hair, but not her mousy shade. It was a beautiful jet black, with *curls*, for God's sake. *Damn growth's hair looks better than mine,* she thought as she stomped through the puddles toward the address Karen had given her.

When she reached it, Melanie thought at first that there was some mistake, that the address was wrong. The building looked like a warehouse, plain brick on the outside, with no sign to indicate its purpose. But then a sudden siren sounded behind her, and she jumped back to avoid a racing ambulance. A door irised open in the side of the building and the vehicle raced inside.

Melanie was left standing in the sudden silence. She slowly approached the spot where the van had disappeared, and found a grate hidden among the brick. Unsure of what to do, she spoke haltingly into the grate. "Uh, excuse me. Is this the hospital?"

For a moment, nothing happened. Then a metallic voice answered coldly, "This is the regional trauma unit. Have you been involved in an accident?"

"Well, no. But I think I'm sick. You treat sick people, don't you?"

"You must be referred by your family physician to be admitted," said the voice.

"But I don't have one," Melanie said. She discovered that her fingernails were cutting into her palms, and forced her hands to relax. Her hands were her livelihood, after all.

"You must have a family physician to be admitted," the voice said, then it went silent.

"Wait, wait, wait!" Melanie screamed, pounding her hand against the grate, tears streaming. Was there no one to help her? Just nameless voices and sims, all designed to add to her torment? As she sobbed, the lump rocked silently back and forth, like a sim that didn't care.

She walked for an hour back to her apartment, unable to stand the stares and insults that went with a tram ride, then locked the door and collapsed in tears on her bed. Supper was unthinkable, but eventually she roused herself to get undressed. In her nightgown, she sat in front of the mirror and stared at her reflection while she brushed her hair. There was no use denying it now. The lump was a head, complete with nose, mouth, ears, and a pair of tightly closed eyes. And all that lovely hair.

Hesitantly, reached up and began to comb the lump's hair. No point having her own hair neat and the other's a tangled mess. Tomorrow was a work day. She prayed hopelessly that the women wouldn't laugh at her.

#

The next day, Melanie came very close to losing her job. She now wore a veil over the lump, but Karen insisted on seeing it. Melanie's fingers almost wouldn't twitch the net aside, but eventually they did.

Karen's eyes opened widely for a moment, then one side of her mouth twitched. "Well," she said. "I guess she'll need a name."

"A *name*?" Melanie nearly shouted. "It's a *lump*, for God's sake." Heads were turning, but she couldn't stop. "A *growth*! It needs to be removed!"

At that moment, the warning bell sounded, and she turned back to the screen, angrily tugging the veil back into place. Karen laughed softly next door. "How about Zaphod?" she suggested softly. Melanie started typing, entering data that was played into her earpiece. The rhythm was soothing, in a way. She knew that she could do this job. She also knew that if she faltered, fell behind, she would be out the door. So, when a message began to thread across her task bar, she kept plugging away only slowing slightly.

"*Read this carefully,*" the message ran. "*It will not be repeated. You are not the first. You must act quickly. There is a doctor you can see.*"

Melanie stopped dead, and watched the screen in disbelief. The words traveled relentlessly across, like a tiny train leaving a tunnel, then entering another, never to reappear. Her earpiece whispered that she had five seconds to resume typing or face termination. Somehow she got through the rest of the day and ran home, locked the door, and lay face down on the bed, sobbing.

There was hope! There was a doctor she could see, but he was not nearby, and she would have to take a medical leave. She had never heard of such a thing, but she discovered that they were all entitled to it. She could not recall anyone ever needing one. Even a rare pregnancy resulted in absences of no more than a week.

The decision was forced on her that night, as she sat stroking her hair, staring past the cracks and trying to avoid looking at the head. Melanie absently began brushing the head's hair, as she always did now. Without warning, the head's eyes flew open, and locked on Melanie's reflection. Melanie moaned. It seemed alert, aware somehow.

Melanie threw her brush at the mirror, and a large piece broke free and smashed to the floor. She could see that it had been held together on the back with masking tape, where no one could see.

"Like my life," she whispered, staring in horror at the starred reflection. "No more." The head had to go, and it had to go *now*.

#

She called in sick the next morning, a strange idea itself, and took a tram out to the city limits. The tram at first was crowded, and she stood in a corner, clutching her overnight bag, watching as normal people went about their normal business. Soon things cleared; most people were headed into the city center. As she sank into a vacant seat, Melanie experienced an odd double vision, bringing on a severe attack of vertigo. Fortunately, after a minute it cleared and didn't return.

At the final stop, she stepped onto an almost deserted platform. Melanie had never left the city, and even this trip would use a large portion of her savings. *And how will I pay the doctor?* she thought briefly. No matter. She would manage. There was only one important thing – to be rid of the growth.

Lurching into motion, Melanie stepped aboard an outbound train, and as she did a scanner read her print so the cost could be deducted from her savings. The trip would take two hours, and lead Melanie into unfamiliar territory, but she had found strength in her hatred for the lump. Determination.

People stared – she had left her veil at home. No matter. They wouldn't understand. She couldn't hide today. Not today. Today was going to be a new beginning.

The train sped through a zone of abandoned and mostly destroyed buildings that surrounded the city, while Melanie watched the rivulets of rain run horizontally across the window pane. The drops split and rejoined, collided with other drops in almost infinite patterns. The trip was over before she was ready to get off.

This town looked very much like home – brick and concrete – and the office was off an alley in back of a convenience store. She would never have found it without directions.

There was only a name stenciled on the mailbox – no sign. Her appointment wasn't for two hours yet, and the door was locked. Probably they're out for lunch, she thought. Or maybe I'm their only appointment today.

Melanie went back around to the convenience store and selected a seafood sub from the machine there. Another extravagance. She almost never ate out. After a moment's hesitation, she added a juice and some sauce. Who knew when she'd get to eat again? There was nowhere to sit, so she went back out front and perched on the curb to eat.

Just as she finished the sub, she had another spell of vertigo, worse than on the train, and when she checked her watch it was nearly her appointment time. As she got up she noticed a teenaged boy across the street. He was staring at her, nodding slowly. Creepy, she thought, and hurried down the alley to the unmarked door. This time it was open.

The door opened on a small warm room with three old chairs. The carpet, the discolored walls, even the furniture, were varying tones of beige. She could hear someone moving about behind the frosted glass of a closed door opposite her. She had been sitting all day, and anyway she felt jumpy, so she stood and waited. Melanie could sense the head next to her. It seemed alert, watching. Her vision doubled for a second and then cleared. *Enjoy the view dear*, Melanie thought savagely.

Shortly the door opened and a man waved her inside. The other room – there seemed to be only two – could not have been more of a contrast from the waiting area. It was all humming electronics and stainless steel. Looking at all the instruments, Melanie felt like she should have showered before entering. The doctor was also clean and crisp in a pressed white lab coat. His skin was a chocolate color, and a surgical mask hung loosely around his neck, although she could see no signs of any recent surgery. He wore one of those lights on his head, like a caricature. Do they actually still use those? Melanie thought absently. His English was good, but a bit clipped.

"Hello, Miss, uh, Terry," he said. "I'm Doctor Parma." She couldn't quite place his accent, but she studied him closely as he introduced himself. He seemed young for a doctor, maybe thirty, but perhaps all doctors were young now.

He smiled reassuringly. "You seem nervous. That is ... understandable. I assure you that I am fully qualified, even though I came to this country only recently, and have been forced to practice in secret. The local authorities have not provided me with a license, for some reason." He leaned forward and said in a low voice, "Perhaps they think you have no need for doctors, eh?" He had the whitest teeth Melanie had ever seen, and she found herself staring at them while he talked. It was hard to concentrate, and her head hurt, so she was content to let him prattle on.

"You needn't be concerned about the surgery," Doctor Parma continued. Melanie could see that he was studying her closely. His eyes flicked constantly back and forth between her and the lump. "For some reason, I have seen several people like you this year. But with modern equipment the surgery is quite simple. It can all be done here in my office, today."

Melanie was not prepared for the rush of relief she felt. Soon the ordeal would all be over. She felt tears welling in her eyes, and opened her mouth to thank the doctor. But she found herself unable to speak. At first she thought it was just emotion, but she was totally mute.

Then she heard a strange voice. A throaty, *sexy* voice. It came from the growth next to her. It said, "Oh, thank you, Doctor. You have no idea what a burden this ... this *thing* has been. Yes, let's get it removed as quickly as possible!"

Melanie Terry felt her body walk toward the surgical table.

Confessions of Me: Betrayer of Humanity

by Zohar A. Goodman

Zohar A Goodman, who rarely writes prose, produces poetry of various lengths (everything from haiku to novellas) containing expressions of direct experience with divine ecstasy & cross-cultural mysticism as well as outright horror and/or erotic & speculative story-poems. He lives in Cleveland, Ohio. His work has most recently appeared in *Walking Bones Magazine, Quill-Pen.net Magazine of Unbelievable Stories, New Genre Magazine, Contemporary Rhyme, Simulacrum Magazine and Forbidden Texts.*

Without warning all humans fell in love unstoppable, *BigLove* inescapable, bigger than anything else plus it felt so flowing fluxing fine (at first) nobody cared if no one knew what it really was, where it really came from, what it really meant. *BigLove* impregnated every organism when it hit – it hit like eternal orgasm brink – from scalp to sole…but so many occupy Ribcage Zoo, random anecdotes must do; then I'll get to me: betrayer of humanity.

#

Five-year-old Tony Lococo was napping in his bedroom shared by baby brother Joe when *BigLove* struck – it woke Tony clean out of his dream, wearing an effortless smile branched beyond bedroom walls – *BigLove* bush-burned Tony's brain, tissue unconsumed.

Across the shag carpet baby Joey cooed angelically. Tony gazed *BigLovingly* at little bro – *God damn it!* a sore memory rushed like racing roaches: Dad's booming crippling voice, *"You screwed up again God damn it you loser bum idiot kid . . ."* The First Time Tony'd heard the words *God damn* WHAP another nasty memory invaded – Dad drunk belting Mom and Tony powerless to prevent it; it was all that baby Joey's fault. Everything was better before that pee-pee sprinkler poo-poo factory came and made Tony's room reek.

Another scary memory surfaced: the dark shark tank at Aquarius Aquarium. Wouldn't it be kewl, Tony darkly fantasized, if one of Dad's razors happened to slice baby Joey's bowleg so blood drooled dripping down to those shadowy waters driving hungry sharks wild…then wouldn't it be superkewl to kick his stinky poopy butt into the tank and watch those razor tooth monsters rip him apart –

A grubby bug-eyed beggar paused his "Spare change? Help the homeless?" chirps to look around in wonder. Everyone on the busy corner was either oblivious to him or avoiding eye-contact all together creating a phantom space for him to not be in. He liked that phantom space: he owned it. When *BigLove* hit – all sprawl paused to notice this unwashed panhandler. Drivers off'd their motors to get out and gape: the beggar their sole center of attention. *BigLove* gushed at the very idea of giving money to the beggar and give they did, lining up – for the simple act of charity intensified *BigLove* to flow even more serenely through their cores and oh that glow rushed fine, d'Vine from Eden River. The grinning beggar accepted all he could, not fighting it as *BigLove* surged to all givers – attracting even more *BigLove* to pour even more Uplink down their heart-core crowns; but this beggar only had two grimy hands and holey pockets it was all going so agonizingly slow… Many who'd already given craved to give more to get more of that fabulous flow. Some shoved back toward the beggar and some who got shoved shoved the hell *back* – sucker punching crotch-kicked slaps back-stabbing choking bites mad haymakers 'round ringed fingers –

The surging brawl waved over the beggar who fell, spine

severing with a sickening snap across the curb – –

\#

    Speaking of snap…
    Before I sucked the Human Whole my brain broke. I want that clearly understood. Behavior comes from the brain, but mine was broken, heartbroken at first. Guilt, guilt, beat my grieving brain. *BigLove* meant nothing to me, all I obsessed on was Miriam: buried on Earth, but I loved her best on Planet Tohu. We were colleagues, interplanetary ethnologists on spaceship Understanding. Our mission? Bridge barriers negatively associated with the divisive word "alien." Tohu's where *BigLove* first un-dammed. I refer you to my spoken notes, way back when (so it seems) I truly wanted to Understand, unlike now, stuck with this bloody brainball shish kabobed atop my spine –

\#

Spoken Notes of: Chester Osterman, Interplanetary Ethnologist
Planet: Tohu   Host Society: Dibi

    I'm not going out there, ohhh no I'm not stepping foot outside this puny hut on the Great Gahba Plain…not at night! My little lamp's the only artificial light on this whole planet – it comforts and accuses me; but I'm staying put till Understanding reenters orbit, God, 84 hours from now.
    Mount Kohlkoh's out there, mighty Kohlkoh in the dark, but I'm not going out there. I admit: I'm currently unable to handle my mission: to observe Dibi culture. *I was* doing fine, learning their mellifluous language, stubbornly sweet character, dewy diet and those deeply concave faces! Dibi features (orangutanian by Earth comparison) appear flat – as though painted on bottoms of empty bowls. When Dibi lovers "kiss" *wyrmph lumphleeplub* they press their hollow heads together – rim to rim – to form a private globe. What goes on inside I've yet to understand, much less experience. Dibi faces are so concave, one wonders where their brains can be!
    Tonight most Dibi "take the walk" *booshevelahktee* to Kohlkoh:

the shiny-black mountain dominating the Great Gahba Plain. I'm graciously invited to participate. Sorry! Not tonight. No *booshevelahktee* for me.

It feels like Kohlkoh's a monstrous dryer...and I'm a dab o'dew.

Physically, Kohlkoh's immense: nine Mount Everests high and 12 Grand Canyons around; but spiritually, exclusively at night (Dibi say) Kohlkoh becomes *kwol yalheem*: a "sacred dimension" they approach on foot (*booshevelahktee*) till they *daht'hah'vahv*: "Uplink" or "leap" to "be the Being" whatever that means, it's my duty to discover, but not tonight, ohhh no.

Mighty Kohlkoh's out there, dominating the dark, overwhelmingly silent...like some colossal god that means me no harm; but I'm not taking the walk, ohhh no. I'm a little uneasy, OK? Maybe some Dibi'll laugh at me come morning, maybe I'll lose some hard-earned respect...oh well! I'm not going out there, that's all.

All Dibi who *booshevelahktee* expect to experience *looahlia*: "divine ecstasy" apparently, pure awareness that triggers "Upleap" or "link" to "be the Being." They claim *looahlia* causes two simultaneous effects: 1) *feshen*: it "sheds surface mind" plus 2) *seyod*: "elevates sacred mind," leaving one *vanuk*: "naked-aware" to be the Being: the grand culmination of *booshevelahktee*, but not for me. I'll be sticking to "surface mind," thanks. Seems I can't shake this crazy notion that surface mind's necessary for sanity. Wrong-headed as this may be, I'm not ready to shed my mind-skin tonight – I'm staying put in my puny hut on the Great Gahba Plain, just me and my lone little lamp...

Hoo wee did I just have an ecstatic experience. It involves peeing, yes, but it's no less profound for that. I had to pee – it happens to humans, but there's no place for that in this or *any* hut on Tohu. Dibi don't pee, you see, nor do they defecate, for that matter. Everything they eat is absorbed, nothing is excreted. How weird I must appear to them, tonight, seated, while they take the walk...

I held it for awhile, but bladder will dominate brain. I *had* to step outside or violate this hut. Haltingly I spread the leathery door-flaps...instantly my vision expanded to boundless darkness. I couldn't see my hand before my zipper –

Standing out there, utterly alone on the Great Gahba Plain, mighty Kohlkoh unseen but overshadowing everything, I simply let it go, effortlessly let it flow – not aiming where I was peeing… and felt it! *Looahlia*: the Dibi ecstatic state. Suddenly nothing occupies my mind save that shiny-black mountain, urging me to *booshevelahktee*. How cramped my puny hut seems now, how dim my little lamp. Is it possible Kohlkoh's shucked *my* surface mind? The fear I felt for sure is gone…I could drop this microphone at any time and . . .

#

So yeah, I took the walk, but I sure didn't "understand." My Homo sapiens brain is convex – compared to Dibi, concave brains. Theirs *contain* consciousness like nests, while my noggin *projects* awareness – hyper-boosted by Kohlkoh? Well, the closer I soled to that monolith the more *BigLove* possessed me, with alien voices surfing my thought-waves. When *I* Uplinked it became immediately obvious: you need no stinkin' spaceship to "reach" Earth. 3D distance means nothing when one projects BigLove from the core I AM all humans share. Kohlkoh and I'd created a *bigger* Bang –

I meant well when I *was* the well where BeingGlow flooded all human beings behind their screens of sense. Talk about fertilizing the Family Tree! I sapped all my "relatives" a deLight gift – sure to give their souls a shift. What they assumed "love" to be was a narrow trickle…I caused ecstasy to triple! Mental moonlights kissed pure sun when *BigLove* beamed on everyOne and those alien voices spurred me on – hijacking my thinker:

"Blameless brain-slave, have no fear. Soon all sense-shells shall be clear…"

"Brain-prism prisonism's a natural disease, like cancer in a limitless lustrous body. Well I AM the tumor remover and I AM the tomb remover too – with nothing but best of intentions for you…"

Best intentions my ass.

I Witnessed <u>all</u> when it went wrong, my Earth world-wonder became King Kong…like Tony's little brother or that beggar's snapped spine – – brain-fruit rotted on *BigLove* vine.

"I and I – " alien voices vibed in my head, "scanners show non-equilibrium planet-wide, neural knots blocking deLight absorption. *BigLove* infusion…unleashing brain-buried agitations…aborting I Mercy mission…"

"Their anger release does not decrease its toxic source, but makes it worse."

Funny…my Uplinked Witness saw all save one: *my own love*! When Miriam (I nicked her Mirror, she called me Chest) shuttled down to Tohu to rescue *me* from Kohlkoh's clutches, she barely noticed *BigLove*. We already shared the infatuated rapture some call chemistry the moment our hearts met : hopelessly harmonized. We adored the odor of one another's skin and thrived on sex – becoming deeper soul-sharers, saying anything and listening openheartedly…

Via Understanding's data, Mirror'd merely hypothesized I was caught in a "quantum vacuum" fluxed from Kohlkoh's energy field. As she hugged me, I suddenly sorely missed the independence sacrificed doing things *she* liked to do. Simultaneously she fret she loved me more than I loved her. She couldn't bear the thought of me leaving, so vowed not to be the *first* one left…that's when Tohu's twin suns dawned and the BigLove flood cut off – but no Noah rainbow. At dawn Kohlkoh flips from spiritual to material; but unlike me or the Dibi, Mirror had NOT *booshevelahktee*'d. Thus, as mighty Kohlkoh switched from 6 to 3D field…she pulverized to bloody ribbons draped over my arms –

Thus ended my stint aboard the Understanding.

On Earth, I felt no "closure" at her funeral. I had no time to say goodbye – to the confidence her mere presence lent me, goodbye to the best sex of my life. The simple joy of seeing her face – cut out of my heart forever. My mind felt wooden, living-dead. Watching TV did no damn good. The screen flashed senseless images and jumbled noise…worst of all the love scenes shoved sharp daggers in my heart –

I shut myself off in my home, muted the phone, narrowed the blinds – didn't want to feel better. If I wasn't suffering every second it could cut my connection to Mirror and everything in the house reminded me of her. I felt so pathetic inside I wanted to look just as pathetic outside and did so quite successfully… till those alien voices returned to Broken Brain Base behind my face.

First came a welcome *ping* between my temples, this soothing *ping* of pure relief, like a fraction of forever that's forever just the same. Who can blame me for basking? I let that ping do its thing. For all I knew it was Miriam nursing sweet relief to my broken brain – like water from Biblical rock. Did that splendorous balm come from my love beyond the grave? No. It did not. It was those aliens with their stinkin' *BigLove*. No way to run from the core of your broken brain, where they washed away the pain. Even when I drew a blank, they saw that just the same. Then in dead of night they voiced a request: for me to work at their behest –

"Your brain-chained relatives reject *BigLove*! Not wholly their fault, locked in brain and body vault. But Chest, with your help, I and I *can* liberate them…"

Hoping to frustrate their interest in me, I blurted an impossible demand: "You want my help? You bring my Mirror back!"

They paused for a second or three…then their reply astonished me:

"Agreed."

They de-valved some sort of dam I guess, infusing me this steady blast of concentrated *ping*. I instantly knew what I had to do: step into my wingtip shoes, grab car keys and go –

3:11 AM's a fun time to rev your motor. At that ungodly hour, under overcast skies, away I went – I never switched my headlights on yet easy-steered those mazy roads clear to my deathstination: Willow Weepin' Cemetery. I parked by the ol' wrought-iron gate, black bars in black night the graveyard's ribs – I was headed for the heart.

Cool graveyard air warmly greeted my face as I soled toward Miriam's grave, forgetting my legs were moving – head hovering – I saw no ghosts save my own broken brain-frame. Headstones stuck up like tongues from Hell. The whole scene seemed to breeze by my motionless I, who knew precisely where to stop and stare: down dark air at her pitch-black grave. I knew I was there like bat radar –

"Like to lie down?" invited the voices.

"Here?" My wingtip tapped her hard headstone, then my weak knees obliged. I lay back on my buried Mirror. I couldn't distinguish my skin from the air it was in, though sense of *her* was downright hot.

"Care to kiss her, Chest? Like raindrops on a window touch?"

"Yes!"

"Make your right hand left and turn around your heart –"

Whirling within, my hands felt like wet mittens and Mirror's face appeared: kissing close. I wondered why it looked so leathery as hungrily we kissed like helpless maggots (oops, meant magnets). Her tongue tasted terrible as putrid chicken livers, but also something sweet in there, where we effortlessly hitched... then those bastards threw some switch and . . .

All the stars came out.

Not the celestial sphere that's normally here. These stars were all around and up and down, individually bound; and in their "ping" places I saw faces: all shocked and grieving by what we were stealing, sucking deLight through our siphoning kiss – we couldn't stop. That *BigLove* flow felt way too great. No way for our "relatives" to halt their fading fate...

At dawn, feeling hung under, I left the cemetery like a guilty ghoul – fully aware I'd been The Enemy's tool. I heard 'em running out on my broken brain:

"I and I: are all brain-slaves free?"

"No. 52% *still* resist *BigLove*. Those are some stubborn sense-shells!"

"Shall they be left behind to die in their own brain-dye?"

"They must be left behind. If they missed *this* kiss, abandon all hope. They hang themselves with their own rope."

"I and I must agree, reluctantly. They're *patriotically* 3D. Love the 48%. Leave the 52. Let BeingSole kick off its shoe -- "

So here I am, stuck with me: betrayer of humanity. One o' the proud 52%ers "left" on Earth; and righteously pissed. Those soul-suckers soothed and seduced me, but dammit they didn't *release* me!

Now all us "low-realmers" are stuck in stinkin' mortal hides. Oh as long as we keep sperm and eggin' humanity'll be. Every baby born is "I" when it points to its chest – so we all must pass the host to reincarnate guest. Now our headstones are our heads; and speaking of headstones, I have to go.

Those alien bastards kept one promise.
My Mirror.
She's waiting for me now.

Forever

by Robert J. Sawyer

> Called "the dean of Canadian science
> fiction" by the *Ottawa Citizen* and
> "just about the best science-fiction
> writer out there" by the *Denver Rocky
> Mountain News*, Robert J. Sawyer is
> one of only sixteen authors in history
> to win the science-fiction field's two
> highest honors: the Nebula Award
> for Best Novel of the Year (which
> he won in 1996 for The Terminal
> Experiment) and the Hugo Award
> for Best Novel of the Year (which
> he won in 2003 for Hominids). He
> has eight other Hugo nominations
> to his credit, and has won nine
> Canadian Science Fiction and Fantasy
> Awards ("Auroras"), an Arthur Ellis
> Award from the Crime Writers of
> Canada, *Analog* magazine's Analytical
> Laboratory Award for Best Short Story
> of the Year, and the *Science Fiction
> Chronicle* Reader Award for Best Short
> Story of the Year. His sixteenth novel,
> Mindscan, was released in 2005
> by Tor, and twenty-two of his forty
> published short stories were recently
> collected as Iterations (Red Deer
> Press).

"Forever" first appeared in Return of the Dinosaurs

*Everything we know about dinosaurs comes from a skewed
sample: the only specimens we have are of animals who happened to die*

at locations in which fossilization could occur; for instance, we have no fossils at all from areas that were mountainous during the Mesozoic.

Also, for us to find dinosaur fossils, the Mesozoic rocks have to be re-exposed in the present day—assuming, of course, that the rocks still exist; some have been completely destroyed through subduction beneath the Earth's crust.

From any specific point in time—such as what we believe to be the final million years of the age of dinosaurs—we have at most only a few hundred square miles of exposed rock to work with. It's entirely possible that forms of dinosaurs wildly different from those we're familiar with did exist, and it's also quite reasonable to suppose that some of these forms persisted for many millions of years after the end of the Cretaceous.

But, of course, we'll never know for sure.

—Jacob Coin, Ph.D.
Keynote Address,
A.D. 2018 Annual Meeting of the
Society of Vertebrate Paleontology

#

Five planets could be seen with the naked eye: Sunhugger, Silver, Red, High, and Slow; all five had been known since ancient times. In the two hundred years since the invention of the telescope, much had been discovered about them. Tiny Sunhugger and bright Silver went through phases, just like the moon did; Red had visible surface features, although exactly what they were was still open to considerable debate. High was banded, and had its own coterie of at least four moons, and Slow – Slow was the most beautiful of all, with a thin ring orbiting around its equator.

Almost a hundred years ago, Ixoor the Scaly had discovered a sixth planet – one that moved around the Sun at a more indolent pace than even Slow did; Slow took twenty-nine years to make an orbit, but Ixoor's World took an astonishing eighty-four.

Ixoor's World – yes, she had named it after herself, assuring her immortality. And ever since that discovery, the search had been on for more planets.

Cholo, an astronomer who lived in the capital city of Beskaltek, thought he'd found a new planet himself, about ten years ago. He'd been looking precisely where Raymer's law predicted an as-yet-undiscovered planet should exist, between the orbits of Red and High. But it soon became apparent that what Cholo had found was nothing more than a giant rock, an orbiting island. Others soon found additional rocks in approximately the same orbit. That made Cholo more determined than ever to continue scanning the heavens each night; he'd rather let a meatscooper swallow him whole than have his only claim to fame be the discovery of a boulder in space ...

He searched and searched and searched, hoping to discover a seventh planet. And, one night, he did find something previously uncatalogued in the sky. His tail bounced up and down in delight, and he found himself hissing "Cholo's world" softly over and over again – it had a glorious sound to it.

But, as he continued to plot the object's orbit over many months, making notes with a claw dipped in ink by the light of a lamp burning sea-serpent oil, it became clear that it wasn't another planet at all.

Still, he had surely found his claim to immortality.

Assuming, of course, that anyone would be left alive after the impact to remember his name.

#

"You're saying this flying mountain will hit the Earth?" said Queen Kava, looking down her long green-and-yellow muzzle at Cholo.

The Queen's office had a huge window overlooking the courtyard. Cholo's gaze was momentarily distracted by the sight of a large, furry winger gliding by. He turned back to the queen. "I'm not completely thirty-six thirty-sixths certain, Your Highness," he said. "But, yes, I'd say it's highly likely."

Kava's tail, which, like all Shizoo tails, stuck straight out behind her horizontally held body, was resting on an intricately carved wooden mount. Her chest, meanwhile, was supported from beneath by a padded cradle. "And what will happen to the Earth when this giant rock hits us?"

Cholo was standing freely; no one was allowed to sit in the presence of the Queen. He tilted his torso backward from the hips, letting the tip of his stiff tail briefly touch the polished wooden floor of the throne room. "Doubtless Your Highness has seen sketches of the moon's surface, as observed through telescopes. We believe those craters were made by the impacts of similar minor planets, long ago."

"What if your flying rock hits one of our cities?"

"The city would be completely destroyed, of course," said Cholo. "Fortunately, Shizoo civilization only covers a tiny part of the globe. Anyway, odds are that it will impact the ocean. But if it does hit on land, the chances are minuscule that it will be in an inhabited area."

The Shizoo lived on an archipelago of equatorial islands. Although many kinds of small animals existed on the islands, the greatest beasts – wild shieldhorns, meatscoopers, the larger types of shovelbills – were not found here. Whenever the Shizoo had tried to establish a colony on the mainland, disaster ensued. Even those who had never ventured from the islands knew of the damage a lone meatscooper or a marauding pack of terrorclaws could inflict.

A nictitating membrane passed in front of Kava's golden eyes. "Then we have nothing to worry about," she said.

"If it hits the land," replied Cholo, "yes, we are probably safe. But if it hits the ocean, the waves it kicks up may overwhelm our islands. We have to be prepared for that."

Queen Kava's jaw dropped in astonishment, revealing her curved, serrated teeth.

#

Cholo predicted they had many months before the flying mountain would crash into the Earth. During that time, the Shizoo built embankments along the perimeters of their islands. Stones had to be imported from the mainland – Shizoo usually built with wood, but something stronger would be needed to withstand the waves.

There was much resistance at first. The tiny dot, visible only in a telescope, seemed so insignificant. How could it pose a threat to the proud and ancient Shizoo race?

But the dot grew. Eventually, it became visible with the naked eye. It swelled in size, night after night. On the last night it was seen, it had grown to rival the apparent diameter of the moon.

\#

Cholo had no way to know for sure when the impact would occur. Indeed, he harbored a faint hope that the asteroid would disintegrate and vaporize in the atmosphere – he was sure that friction with the air was what caused shooting stars to streak across the firmament. But, of course, Cholo's rock was too big for that.

The sound of the asteroid's impact was heard early in the morning – a great thunderclap, off in the distance. But Cholo knew sound took time to travel – it would take three-quarters of a day for a sound to travel halfway around the world.

Most of the adult population had stayed up, unable to sleep. When the sound did come, some of the Shizoo hissed in contempt. A big noise; that was all. Hardly anything to worry about. Cholo had panicked everyone for no good reason; perhaps his tail should be cut off in punishment ...

But within a few days, Cholo was vindicated – in the worst possible way.

The storms came first – great gale-force winds that knocked down trees and blew apart huts. Cholo had been outdoors when the first high winds hit; he saw wingers crumple in the sky, and barely made it to shelter himself, entering a strongly built wooden shop.

A domesticated shieldhorn had been wandering down the same dirt road Cholo had been on; it dug in its four feet, and tipped its head back so that its neck shield wouldn't catch the wind. But five of its babies had been following along behind it, and Cholo saw them go flying into the air like so many leaves. The shieldhorn opened her mouth and was doubtless bellowing her outrage, but not even the cry of a great crested shovelbill would have been audible over the roar of this storm.

The wind was followed by giant waves, which barreled in

toward the Shizoo islands; just as Cholo had feared, the asteroid had apparently hit the ocean.

The waves hammered the islands. On Elbar, the embankments gave way, and most of the population was swept out to sea. Much damage was done to the other islands, too, but – thank the Eggmother! – overall, casualties were surprisingly light.

It was half a month before the seas returned to normal; it was even longer before the heavens completely cleared. The sunsets were spectacular, stained red as though a giant meatscooper had ripped open the bowl of the sky.

#

"You have done the Shizoo people a great service," said Queen Kava. "Without your warning, we would all be dead." The monarch was wearing a golden necklace; it was the only adornment on her yellowish-gray hide. "I wish to reward you."

Cholo, whose own hide was solid gray, tilted his head backward, exposing the underside of his neck in supplication. "Your thanks is reward enough." He paused, then lowered his head. "However ..."

Kava clicked the claws on her left hand against those on her right. "Yes?"

"I wish to go in search of the impact site."

The waves had come from the west. Dekalt – the continent the Shizoo referred to as "the mainland" – was to the east. There was a land mass to the west, as well, but it was more than five times as far away. Shizoo boats had sailed there from time to time; fewer than half ever returned. There was no telling how far away the impact site was, or if there would be anything to see; the crater might be completely submerged, but Cholo hoped its rim might stick up above the waves.

Queen Kava flexed her claws in surprise. "We are recovering from the worst natural disaster in our history, Cholo. I need every able body here, and every ship for making supply runs to the mainland." She fell silent, then: "But if this is what you want ..."

"It is."

Kava let air out in a protracted hiss. "It's not really a suitable reward. Yes, you may have the use of a ship; I won't deny you that. But while on your voyage, think of what you really want – something lasting, something of value."

"Thank you, Your Highness," said Cholo. "Thank you."

Kava disengaged her tail from the wooden mount, stepped away from her chest cradle, and walked over to the astronomer, placing the back of a hand, her claws bent up and away, gently on his shoulder. "Travel safely, Cholo."

#

They sailed for almost two months without finding any sign of the impact site. Cholo had tried to determine the correct heading based on the apparent direction from which the huge waves had come, plus his knowledge of the asteroid's path through the sky, but either he had miscalculated, or the ocean really had covered over all evidence of the impact. Still, they had come this far; he figured they might as well push on to the western continent.

The ship deployed its anchor about thirty-six bodylengths from the shore, and Cholo and two others rowed in aboard a small boat. The beach was covered with debris obviously washed in by giant waves – mountains of seaweed, millions of shells, coral, driftwood, several dead sea serpents, and more. Cholo had a hard time walking over all the material; he almost lost his balance several times.

The scouting party continued on, past the beach. The forest was charred and blackened – a huge fire had raged through here recently, leaving burnt-out trunks and a thick layer of ash underfoot. The asteroid would have heated up enormously coming through the atmosphere; even if it did hit the ocean, the air temperature might well have risen enough to set vegetation ablaze. Still, there were already signs of recovery: in a few places, new shoots were poking up through the ash.

Cholo and his team hiked for thousands of bodylengths. The crew had been looking forward to being on solid ground again, but there was no joy in their footsteps, no jaunty bouncing of tails; this burned-out landscape was oppressive.

Finally, they came to a river; its waters had apparently held back the expanding fire. On the opposite side, Cholo could see trees and fields of flowers. He looked at Garsk, the captain of the sailing ship. Garsk bobbed from her hips in agreement. The river was wide, but not raging. Cholo, Garsk, and three others entered its waters, their tails undulating from side to side, their legs and arms paddling until they reached the opposite shore.

As Cholo clambered up the river's far bank and out onto dry land, he startled a small animal that had been lurking in the underbrush.

It was a tiny mammal, a disgusting ball of fur.

Cholo had grown sick of sea serpent and fish on the long voyage; he was hoping to find something worth killing, something worth eating.

After about a twelfth of a day spent exploring, Cholo came across a giant shieldhorn skull protruding from the ground. At first he thought it was a victim of the recent catastrophe, but closer examination revealed the skull was ancient—hundreds, if not thousands, of years old. Shizoo legend said that long ago great herds of shieldhorns had roamed this continent, their footfalls like thunder, their facial spears glaring in the sunlight, but no one in living memory had seen such a herd; the numbers had long been diminishing.

Cholo and Garsk continued to search.

They saw small mammals.

They saw birds.

But nowhere did they see any greater beasts. At least, none that were still alive.

At one point, Cholo discovered the body of a meatscooper. From its warty snout to the tip of its tail, it measured more than four times as long as Cholo himself. When he approached the body, birds lifted into the air from it, and clouds of insects briefly dispersed. The stench of rotting meat was overpowering; the giant had been dead for a month or more. And yet there were hundreds of stoneweights worth of flesh still on the bones. If there had been any mid-sized scavengers left alive in the area, they would have long since picked the skeleton clean.

"So much death," said Garsk, her voice full of sadness.

Cholo bobbed in agreement, contemplating his own mortality.

#

Months later, Cholo at last returned to Queen Kava's chambers.

"And you found no great beasts at all?" said the Queen.

"None."

"But there are lots of them left on the mainland," said Kava. "While you were away, countless trips were made there to find wood and supplies to repair our cities."

"'Lots' is a relative term, Your Highness. If the legends are to be believed – not to mention the fossil record – great beasts of all types were much more plentiful long ago. Their numbers have been thinning for some time. Perhaps, on the eastern continent, the aftermath of the asteroid was the gizzard stone that burst the thunderbeast's belly, finishing them off."

"Even the great may fall," said the Queen.

Cholo was quiet for a time, his own nictitating membranes dancing up and down. Finally, he spoke: "Queen Kava, before I left, you promised me another reward – whatever I wanted – for saving the Shizoo people."

"I did, yes."

"Well, I've decided what I'd like ..."

#

The unveiling took place at noon six months later, in the large square outside the palace. The artist was Jozaza – the same Jozaza who had assured her own immortality through her stunning frieze on the palace wall depicting the Eggmother's six hunts.

Only a small crowd gathered for the ceremony, but that didn't bother Cholo. This wasn't for today – it was for the ages. It was for immortality.

Queen Kava herself made a short speech – there were many reasons why Kava was popular, and her brevity was certainly one of them. Then Jozaza came forward. As she turned around to face the audience, her tail swept through a wide arc. She made a much longer speech; Cholo was growing restless, hopping from foot to foot.

Finally the moment came. Jozaza bobbed her torso at four of her assistants. They each took hold of part of the giant leather sheet, and, on the count of three, they pulled it aside, revealing the statue.

It was made of white marble veined with gold that glistened in the sunlight. The statue was almost five times life size, rivaling the biggest meatscooper's length. The resemblance to Cholo was uncanny – it was him down to the very life; no one could mistake it for anyone else. Still, to assure that the statue fulfilled its purpose for generations to come, Cholo's name was carved into its base, along with a description of what he'd done for the Shizoo people.

Cholo stared up at the giant sculpture; the white stone was almost painfully bright in the glare of the sun.

A statue in his honor – a statue bigger than any other anywhere in the world. His nictitating membranes danced up and down.

He *would* be remembered. Not just now, not just tomorrow. He would be remembered for all time. A million years from now – nay, a hundred million hence, the Shizoo people would still know his name, still recall his deeds.

He would be remembered forever.

Sum of their Parts

by Stephanie Bedwell-Grime

Five-time Aurora Award finalist,
Stephanie Bedwell-Grime is the
author of seven published novels
and over fifty short stories. Her
most recent releases are Guardian
Angel and Fallen Angel from
Telos Publishing (www.telos.
co.uk), and The Bleeding Sun
and Wishful Thinking from New
Concepts Publishing (www.
newconceptspublishing.com).
Stephanie's website is:
www.feralmartian.com

"The Sum of Their Parts" originally appeared in NorthWords, Fall 1996

Seven hundred and twenty-three days to go. Zachary Stanton stroked a red line through the date on his desk calendar. Running a hand through his sandy blond hair, he rose wearily from his desk and turned off the lights in the classroom.

He wasn't cut out to be a Kindergarten teacher, he reflected for the millionth time. Criminals, however, had few rights. But the elimination of women left a void in the work force, and it fell to those who had broken society's rules to make up for that gap. Seven years was a stiff punishment, far in excess of the money he'd embezzled. But it could be worse, he reflected grimly, he could be wiping butts in the infirmary. Tomorrow he had to take the boys to see the wombs as part of the obligatory show and tell on where babies came from. Could butt brigade really be worse?

\#

Jacob, the cherubic troublemaker peered into the glass

enclosure at the two-inch fetus and pronounced it "yucky". Zach, who was of the opinion that a fetus wasn't human until at least age twenty-five, had to agree with him. The flexi-plast domes, with their snake's nests of tubes that pumped nutrient rich blood into the forming boy, always made him queasy. When they returned to the classroom he would have to explain the facts of life, which of course would prompt a history lesson on the distasteful topic of women, accompanied by embarrassed giggles from the five year-old boys.

Still red faced, he arrived home in a foul mood, growing fouler by the minute, to find a week's worth of dirty dishes in the sink, a foot of dust on the floor, and his cell mate, Ramon Medeiros, waist deep in the hall circuit panel.

"Damned auto-clean's busted again," Ramon growled, followed by a string of obscenities in Spanish.

"Need a hand?" Zach asked, hoping for a polite refusal.

A shower of sparks sputtered into the hallway, followed by a yelp and curse from Ramon. A dark, sweat-streaked face appeared over the rim of the auto-clean. "What's it look like man? 'Course I need a hand."

#

MERCHANT BANK CLOBBERS METROBANK! read the headline of the morning paper. The story was accompanied by a full colour holo of the blood-covered, late bank president. About time, Zach thought. Merchant Bank had been planning a corporate takeover for weeks. The resulting uncertainty only served to drive the lending rates up. It was long past time the presidents stepped into the ring and settled things man to man.

Corporate Rivalry was the biggest game ever to sweep the country. Big egos, big money was at stake in the ultimate battle for total financial domination. His grandfather was old enough to remember when such things had been regulated by law. Government safety nets only served to coddle the weak. Society had broken down regardless. Now the strong ran the government. The strongest ran the biggest companies.

Apparently the financial community also favoured the takeover. Mortgage rates, for the privileged few who could afford their own cubicles, were dropping.

"Lotta good that does us," Ramon remarked, glancing at the headline while he fumbled about sleepily trying to make coffee by hand. Suspiciously, he eyed Zach. "Why are you in such a good mood?"

"Weekend pass." Zach helped himself to some of Ramon's coffee.

His cellmate grunted. "I've got another year to go before I even get that."

Ramon's characteristic impatience was his downfall. He should have made sure his support network was firmly in place before he ran in with a machine gun in an aborted corporate coup. That ill-planned, ill-timed, impulsive act led to a sentence of ten years in the typing pool.

"As I tell the little terrors at school, crime doesn't pay," Zach said as much to himself as to his cellmate.

Ramon shot him a dark look. Grumbling, he wandered off to boil water for a bath. Zachary flipped through the three sports sections to the news section at the back and stopped cold.

BREEDING CENTER DESTROYED IN FREAK BLAST!

With the eerie feeling of man who'd just escaped his own doom, he read the story. A rival pharmaceutical company was claiming responsibility. Further retaliations were expected. The blast had occurred only minutes after he'd left with the class. While he was walking the floors above, a bomb had been ticking away contentedly in the basement. "Jesus," he whispered, staring at the holos of charred bodies found in the wreck. "That could have been me."

#

As a free man for the next forty-eight hours, he was entitled to visit the Big Bang, as long as he didn't indulge in drugs or alcohol.

An hour later, he was thrusting desperately into the plasti-maiden, his pelvis pressed hard against the flexi-plast, and his hands grasping hungrily at the warm, rubbery breasts. Fifteen seconds of bliss, and the highlight of the weekend would be over. But just as his passion began building toward release, a sudden vision of that collected sperm being sucked down the tubes to keep on ice at the Breed Center made him lose his stride. And further reflection on the disaster he'd so narrowly missed made the coffee churn threateningly in his stomach.

Near misses bothered him. The last time he'd tempted fate, he'd been arrested.

Frustrated, he paid the hundred and fifty dollars and gave up on pleasures of the flesh. His wallet considerably lighter, and alcohol off limits, he settled for soda and watched the flashing vid screens with half his attention.

Seven hundred and twenty-two days to go. Would he even be sane by the end of it? Bitterly, he envisioned himself staggering through the front doors of the school on that last day and promptly having himself committed to the nearest loony bin.

Grimly belaboring that image, he watched a replay of last night's bank match and managed a half-hearted whistle when the Metrobank president went down in a pool of his own blood. The rest went by in a blur, but he tuned in long enough to realize he'd lost another twenty bucks in the hockey pool. His much looked-forward-to weekend was turning into a depressing and expensive waste of time. It would be at least another year before the next, he thought miserably, standing to leave. Just then, the sports were uncharacteristically interrupted by a news flash. Hisses broke out around the bar.

Zach motioned for the bartender to turn up the volume. The guy threw him a look that announced "patsy", but the ten he slapped down on the bar seemed to change his mind.

"...a spokesman for Ovulox has estimated the damage in the billion dollar range. It is not known when production will resume. This is the third attack on a Breed Center this week, as rival companies battle it out over what seems to have started as a hostile stock takeover. Widespread damage to plants in Russia, Saudi Arabia and China have also been reported. The effect on the birth rate can only be speculated at this point, rumors of a world-wide ovum crisis abound..."

The shot zoomed in on the still smoking, gutted remains of the factory, then winked out as the sports commentary resumed.

#

"What's with you?" Ramon demanded when he got a look at Zach's long face. "Didn't you have a good weekend?"

"No, I didn't, if you must know," Zach growled back, which seemed to please Ramon no end.

Suddenly cheerful, Ramon whistled as he dialed breakfast. Fixing the autochef must have been his project for the weekend. "By the way, your parole officer called while you were away. He wants to see you in his office at five tonight."

"Something to look forward to after a hard day," Zach groaned sarcastically, deciding the cards of fate were definitely stacked against him.

Ramon grinned and reached for the paper. "I hope you were a good boy this weekend."

Zach scowled. "I certainly didn't have any fun, if that's what you're hinting at. Legal or otherwise."

#

Knowing what was waiting for him at the end of the day only made the hours pass painfully slowly and the boys' hijinx grate more cuttingly on his nerves. In the end, he gave up on his carefully prepared lessons and surrendered to chaos. By the time the bell sounded, he was almost looking forward to a session with his parole officer. Almost.

His parole officer, a disagreeable sort with a perpetual frown, was all smiles that evening. Zach wondered at this sudden change in temperament and decided he didn't like it at all.

"Zach," he said, as if greeting a long lost chum. "Come in, sit down."

Zachary took the offered seat and crossed his legs nervously.

"Would you like a drink?"

The question shocked him to awareness. "As a convict, I'm well aware that consuming alcohol is beyond my right," he replied carefully.

"Relax Zach," his parole officer said, and smiled some more. The expression was so unusual Zach wondered if the effort might crack his face. "This is a special day."

"It is?"

The parole officer positively beamed. "You're about to become a free man."

As an old teacher had once warned him, there was no such

thing as a free lunch. Nor a free parole. "To what do I owe this unexpected change in plans?"

"Fate," his parole officer answered, pouring him the first bourbon he'd had in eight years. "One man's misfortune is another's gain." He stared at Zach pointedly over his glass. "No doubt you've heard of the attacks on the Breed Centers?"

Zach took a sip of the forbidden bourbon. "What's that got to do with me?"

#

"They want you to do what?" Ramon asked incredulously.

"They want to use me in some sort of breeding experiment," Zach repeated patiently.

"You call that punishment?" Ramon glared at him, then added petulantly, "You have all the luck."

#

The research center reminded Zachary of an anthill. Five rambling floors staffed by officious, identical drones, he imaged the cutaway view would fit right into an entomology textbook.

White coated technicians took down all his vital signs and drew samples of each bodily fluid. By the time they finished he'd accumulated a stack of printouts that approached novel proportions. Zach, who could only think of two possible categories for human beings, alive or dead, was intrigued as well as insulted. But the symbols on the paper were illegible to everyone except the white coats.

His quarters were smaller than the cell he'd shared with Ramon. He suspected the scenic holos that passed for windows were actually two-way mirrors. How else were they going to make sure he followed their endless list of instructions, took his vitamins and didn't engage in any recreational wanking. As if it hadn't been painfully clear before, the state now owned him flesh, blood and gonads. He felt like a prized bull being hired out for stud.

Seven days into his confinement inaction spurred him to hot-wired restlessness. He paced, he drummed his fingers on the chrome tables, he attacked the weight room, bench-pressed one-eighty and still felt uneasy. Finally, he threw himself down onto the cot and turned on the television.

The first ten channels were scrambled, reserved for those who could afford virtual reality porn. The wrestling channel didn't interest him and the hockey game on HNIC was dragging at 0:0. Basketball wasn't his game, and golf and tennis bored him. Baseball managed to hold his flagging interest for nearly thirty minutes before he threw the remote down in disgust and stabbed the call button with the sum of his frustration.

The bored looking white-coat regarded him politely. "Can I help you sir?"

Zach meant to answer the question with the same dull courtesy, but anger grabbed hold of his tongue. "You could tell me what I'm doing here!" Sanity roared in his mind that he might be jeopardizing his parole, but the anger was already unleashed.

White-coat shot him a look of patronizing interest. "I'll inform the coordinator of your concern," he droned and left.

Zach heaved the remote at the television screen and watched with scant satisfaction as it burst into pieces.

In moments the auto-clean had dispensed the vacuum robot and taken care of the mess.

Without the remote, the television was stuck on the baseball channel and the volume on max. He waited patiently for a white-coat to show up and turn it off, but no one came. The noise was starting to get on his already frayed nerves and made sleeping out of the question.

Eventually, he fell into an exhaustion-induced slumber, only to be awakened by cheering crowds at each home run.

#

Sounds of roaring silence awoke him. The yellow glow of the holo on the east wall told him morning had arrived.

"Good Morning!" The auto-orderly rolled into his cubicle, deposited his breakfast, and grated cheerfully in its metallic voice, "You have a 10:30 appointment with Dr. Trahern."

#

They hustled him down the featureless, white halls to a door marked 'TRAHERN'. No 'Doctor' before it. Of course, at the center everyone was a doctor of some sort.

"Something is bothering you?" Trahern asked before Zach had a chance to settle into his chair.

"Bothering me?" Zach forced himself to be as blandly polite as the doctor. "It couldn't be because you show me less courtesy than the rats in your lab and lock me away like one of your bloody housekeeping robots until you find a use for me."

"Now Mr. Stanton..." Trahern's tone warned against further sarcasm. "Surely you realize the details of this experiment are classified. That is necessary for your protection as well as ours."

"Let me guess," Zach said, tying to keep the sarcasm from his voice. "It has something to do with the attacks on the breed centers. Doesn't take a genius to figure that out."

Trahern watched him in owlish silence. "The damage is much more widespread than was reported by what passes for news these days..."

The same infuriating, quiet stare. Surely he'd have to blink some time, Zach thought angrily. And then again, maybe genetic engineers didn't have to." The fate of the entire human race is at stake," he said, testing his theory.

That almost got a smile from Trahern. "Now let's not be melodramatic, Mr. Stanton. The situation is nowhere near as dire as all that. Let's just say we've been forced to return to 'older' technology for the moment."

"Older technology?" Zachary repeated. He'd convinced himself he was desperate enough to do anything to win his freedom, now he wasn't so sure. B-movie scenarios flashed through his mind. He pictured a wild-haired scientist bending over a table where the parts of a woman were being assembled. Lightning flashed overhead. The scientist gasped and stepped back in horror. The patchwork bride rose from the table and pointed her finger at Zach. He thrust his over-active imagination back into a safe compartment in his mind. "Surely you're not thinking of recreating...women?" he asked before he could stop himself from asking such an absurd question.

"Of course not. We wouldn't ask you to do anything that repugnant. You're only serving time for a white-collar crime. It's not like you committed murder. There haven't been females in our society for over one hundred years. We have no desire to reconceive them. They were, after all, unclean, unpredictable, and required only for the breeding of sons. All we really need are their useful parts."

"We *do* teach history in the lower grades," Zach snapped. "Actually, no one knows for sure when they disappeared. There were no records of births and deaths."

Before Trahern had a chance to explain further, the building shook with a force that rattled its foundations deep within the earth. The sound of metal tearing ripped through the halls, louder than a monster truck collision at the coliseum.

Zach, who knew better than most how to turn a problem into an opportunity, took advantage of the situation and fled. The last thing he saw as he dove through the door to Trahern's office was the doctor pinned mid-leap as the ceiling caved in on him.

Bomb, he thought, dodging an avalanche of falling ceiling tile. He wondered if there wasn't some godly puppeteer pulling his strings toward certain disaster.

The halls were chaos, everyone desperately trying to save their own skin. In seconds, he'd lost track of direction. Ceiling became floor; walls crumbled around him. It was like trying to run on the back of a snake.

He barreled through the metal doors ahead, ignoring the shower of debris that rained down his back. If this was the wrong direction, too bad, the alternatives had just disappeared in a hail of rubble.

Panting, he leaned against the wall to get his bearings. The floor rumbled threateningly. Before him glass tanks stretched out in uniform rows across the cavernous room. On the far side a red exit sign still glowed. Zach breathed a sigh of relief and started tentatively toward it.

Two steps. The building trembled again. Lights flickered, a curtain of dust fell into the tanks.

Zach froze, hands gripping the side of the tank and tried to decide whether it was safer to run along the wall or make a diagonal dash across the center of the room. And then, for some reason he was never able to fathom, he looked down at the tank's contents.

It didn't take an anatomy expert to recognize the disembodied womb that lay in the gelatinous cradle of plasma. Not the clear, flexiplast spheres on display on the floors above. These were flesh and blood, the last remains of the female gender.

"Older technology," he muttered, choking back the urge to puke.

Beneath his feet, the building shuddered. Another hit.

The ceiling buckled, the lights went out.

He leapt in what he thought was the direction of the exit, clumsy in the sudden darkness. Another hit brought him to his knees, skidding through broken glass. His hands slid into warm, rubbery flesh. He screamed, trying not to think of the contents of those tanks. Ignoring the pain in his wounded hands, he forced his legs beneath him once again and ran for the far wall.

The wall reared up much before he expected it to. The collision knocked the breath from his lungs. With torn hands he felt desperately for the door. His stinging fingers closed around the cold metal handle. He yanked it open and saw daylight up ahead.

#

Zachary leaned against the plasti-maiden's metal frame. "So how's it going?"

Ramon swore and glared at him over the plasti-babe's mountainous boobs. "You picked one hell of a time for a chat, Zach."

"Wanna hurry it up buddy?" yelled an impatient patron from the line behind. "I've been waiting an hour and a half already!"

"Yeah, you lovers can talk later," growled another.

"I wouldn't want to ruin the highlight of your year." Zach tried desperately to keep the smirk off his face. "Meet me upstairs when you're done. I'll buy you dinner."

Ramon moaned something in the affirmative, and Zach wandered off, nursing his beer.

Fifteen minutes later a much-renewed Ramon appeared. From the way he peered out sleepily from under lowered lids, Zach guessed he'd also sprung for a hot shower and a two-minute massage from the auto-hand.

He looked down at the pressed-meat burger and fries Zach had ordered and grinned. "Thanks."

"It's the least I could do."

"Six hundred and fifty-eight days to go," Ramon said around a mouthful of burger. "What's it like in the free world? I'm not sure I remember."

"Suits me fine."

Ramon glowered at him and swallowed. "Yeah, I bet." He quaffed a mouthful of synthi-beer. "Was it worth it?"

"Aside from nearly getting killed, it wasn't so bad."

Folding his hands like he was in church, Ramon eyed Zach with glee. "So tell me the gory details."

"About the bomb?"

"Not the bomb, stupid. What they wanted you to do."

Zach looked over his shoulder. Satisfied there was no one in the immediate vicinity, and the noise level was enough to absorb anything less than a shout at close range, he leaned across the table and said quietly, "I don't know."

"What d'you mean you don't know?"

"The bomb went off just as I was about to find out."

His former cellmate sat back in his chair. "So you never...you son of a bitch!" He whistled appreciatively. "What if they find out?"

"Find out what? The place was reduced to a smoking crater."

"You're one lucky bastard."

"Don't be such a poor sport," Zach said, with a grin. "You've got less than two years left. And besides, according to the rumors I hear, the damage to the breed centers was so extensive we might be the last generation of men on the earth. But, I'm sure someone somewhere is working on a solution." He winked at his buddy. "You might be called upon yet to do your duty to your country."

"Fat chance that," Ramon said, and changed the subject. "So what you doing these days?"

"Teaching."

"You're shitting me."

"'Fraid not."

"Tell me it's not kindergarten." The indignation held overtones of pity.

"History actually." Zach found himself talking into the silence that followed. "I just couldn't go back to the stock market, not after all I'd seen. I found myself wondering what came before and how we got ourselves into..." he gestured to the pleasure bar around them, "this."

For once Ramon had no witty retort. They stared at each other, the pulse of the music throbbing between them.

"They really screwed up your mind, didn't they?" he said finally.

"Perhaps they did."

Ramon looked around nervously. "Well I gotta go. Thanks for dinner." He stood up too fast. "Have a nice life."

"Be seeing you," Zach said, though he much doubted it.

He gazed at the ever-lengthening line up for the plasti-maiden's synthi-pleasures. Maybe later, he thought, and ordered himself another beer.

Walter's Brain

by Kimberly Footit

Originally from out West, Kimberly
Foottit has lived in Ontario for the
last fifteen years. She has an Honours
BA in history from McMaster
University, but her first love is
writing, having been obsessed by
the craft since the age of eleven. Kim
currently resides in the west end of
Hamilton with her cat, Ben.

"Walter's Brain" was originally published in Hammered Out #7.5

"Lot number 49, Schism, Marshall," Walter Wyndham began, checking
to see if his words appeared on the screen to his right. rBorn: March
30th, 1973. Deceased: October 4th, 2013." He continued to read
the information off the lid of the container in front of him. Height,
weight, education, occupation, social status, marital status, offspring
and cause of death. At this last bit of data, Walter ran his thumb
across the label. It smudged. "Note to Carl in Processing: please use
permanent pigment in the new label printer. Thank you."

Walter knew before opening the container that this specimen
would offer little viable information. A fatal blow to the head with
an axe could do that. Nevertheless, he snapped on a pair of sterile
gloves before removing the grey, jellied mass and placing it on the
scale. Schism, Marshall was weighed, measured and a photo was
taken of the large gash that stretched across both the frontal lobes.
Electrodes were placed in the key areas, but little activity resulted.
Schism, Marshall was disconnected, plopped back into the container
and put out with the daily refuse.

It was another day at the Laboratory for the Study of

Antiquities: Organics Division where technicians spent their time recording information from the past gathered from the brains of the deceased. Walter was firmly ensconced in his office, although his was only an entry level position. While others whizzed past him towards promotions, he was happy studying the memories of everyday people. It wasn't a prestigious job – all that went to the Specialty Office where the brains of the rich, famous, genius and athletic were processed – yet he liked it just the same. Unlike his colleagues, he found the average person far more interesting than the privileged. Walter's last partner hadn't stayed long enough for him to remember his name. He didn't mind. He preferred solitude.

Walter spent the morning cataloging the remembrances of Thayer, Rosemarie and Pindar Joseph. After a lunch spent under the last oak tree on the Laboratory grounds, Walter checked over old files before moving onto the next specimen.

"Lot number 53, Barone, Frances. Born: June 20th, 1975. Deceased: December 10th, 2036. Height: 5'10". Weight: 150lbs. Education: Bachelor of Arts Degree from McMaster University (now McMaster/DeGroote Research Facility). Occupation: Preschool Administrator (retired). Middling Level. Married. Three children. Cause of Death: Accidental Electrocution." Walter paused. He would have to talk to his superiors about the guys in Processing. First a fatal head wound and now a fried brain.

He was surprised, however, when he opened the container and didn't find a grey jellied mass. Barone, Frances' brain was pink as though fresh from the morgue. When Walter placed it onto the scale it jiggled like a firm jello mold. Weighed and measured, it was larger and heavier than the average female brain. Curious, he hooked up the electrodes and flipped the switch.

The machines went crazy. So much data flashed across the screen Walter couldn't make sense of it. The readings were off the charts. Then it slowed down. Then it stopped altogether. Walter took deep breaths, calming his scattered nerves with a logical explanation.

Must have been a left over surge from the original cause of death, he thought as he removed his glasses and rubbed his eyes. Then he froze and stared at the word on the screen.

HELLO?

Walter blinked. The word appeared again.

HELLO?

Walter checked his glasses before putting them on.

HELLO?

He made a mental note to have his prescription checked and perhaps see one of the doctors in the Lab clinic. This had to be a hallucination.

HELLO? IS ANYONE THERE?

"Hello?" Walter didn't realize he had spoken until he saw his response come up on the screen.

OH, YOU'RE THERE. GOOD. FOR A MOMENT I THOUGHT I WAS TALKING TO MYSELF. MY NAME IS FRANCES.

"Walter."

NICE TO MEET YOU WALTER. TELL ME, WHAT YEAR IS IT?

"Year?"

YES. WHAT YEAR IS IT?

Walter paused.

IT'S NOT A TRICK QUESTION.

"I realize that," Walter began, yet he wasn't sure of how to respond to her query.

CAN I BE DIRECT, WALTER? I'M DEAD. WE BOTH KNOW YOU'RE TALKING TO MY BRAIN. THERE'S NO NEED TO PROTECT ME.

Walter knew he was alone, yet he still turned to make sure. He decided it wouldn't do any harm if he told her. Especially since this was all a hallucination anyway.

"2196."

AND WHAT YEAR DID I DIE?

"You don't remember?"

IT'S STILL A LITTLE FUZZY.

"2026." He did the calculations in his head. "You were fifty-one."

HMMMM. There was a pause. AND HOW OLD ARE YOU, IF YOU DON'T MIND ME ASKING?

"I'm thirty-five." Walter pushed his glasses back to the bridge of his nose with shaking hands. Sometime in the last minute he had begun to sweat – a typical nervous reaction for him. He tried to rationalize the situation. He was having a conversation with a dead brain. And not just any brain. A brain who knew it was dead. A brain who would have had to know about his job over 150 years before it had existed. It could only be a case of an ordinary brain with extraordinary functions. One of those office legends one heard about, but never saw. Walter knew he should disconnect Barone, Frances from the machine, pack her up and send her to the Specialty Office. He knew he should, but –

WALTER, ARE YOU STILL THERE?

"Yes."

TELL ME ABOUT THIS PLACE. WHERE ARE WE? WHO DO YOU WORK FOR?

Rather than think about his situation, Walter spent the next hour focused on answering all of her questions. The alarm on his watch signaled quitting time.

"It's quitting time."

OH. NOW WHAT HAPPENS?

"Well I can't leave you out. Even if you didn't dry up, the cleaning staff comes in here at night. They'd report that the machines were still on." He turned around and looked at the wall of cabinets behind him. "And I can't put you in back in the cabinet."

WHY NOT?

"They automatically lock after a specimen is removed so Processing knows which ones to fill."

OH.

Walter turned back and remembered the small fridge in the outer office. The last occupant of the outer office had left for the bigger world beyond years ago and a replacement was never hired. *That just might work.*

"I have an idea. I'll have to unhook you now," he said.

WALTER?

"Yes."

YOU WILL COME BACK, WON'T YOU? IT'S NICE TO HAVE SOMEONE TO TALK TO. IT'S BEEN LONELY.

Walter hesitated. He knew he should pack her up. He knew things could get complicated if he didn't.

For the first time in his life, Walter broke the rules. "I promise."

#

He had been up half the night trying to analyze what

had happened that day. Machine malfunctions, hallucination, simultaneously? It was a bit out of range for him logically, but it had finally helped him sleep. He planned to run full machine diagnostics and visit the Lab clinic the following day.

His diagnostics came up normal and his mind drifted back to the fridge in the outer office.

The log on lot 55 – Quest, Wendell – was completed when he could no longer avoid temptation.

Before he could talk himself out of it, Walter was in the outer office, reaching for the fridge door handle. The container was exactly where he had left it on the top shelf. Waiting.

WALTER?

He had barely secured the electrodes and she was already there.

"Yes, Frances, I'm here." He smiled a little as he used her name.

FOR A MOMENT I THOUGHT YOU WEREN'T COMING BACK.

"Why wouldn't I?"

HOW MANY OTHER BRAINS HAVE COMMUNICATED WITH YOU SINCE YOU BEGAN THIS JOB?

"Um, none."

EXACTLY.

"I promised I'd come back."

BUT...?

"But what?"

COME ON WALTER, I MAY BE DEAD, BUT I'M NOT STUPID. WHAT'S GOING ON?

"Nothing."

WALTER, ONE THING FRIENDS NEVER DO IS LIE TO EACH OTHER.

Friends? Walter pushed up his glasses as he began to sweat again. She had called them friends. "Well, this isn't exactly a regular occurrence," he said aloud.

AND WHAT DO YOU DO WHEN SOMETHING IRREGULAR OCCURS?

"I'm supposed to report it to my superiors. You should be packed up and sent to the Specialty Office for further analysis."

WELL, YOU CAN REPORT IT ANYTIME. I WON'T SAY A

THING.

He paused, fiddling with his glasses, still sweating.

WALTER?

WALTER?

"What?" His voice sounded very small to his own ears.

WHAT DO YOU WANT TO DO?

"I don't know."

YES YOU DO.

Walter struggled with his conscience. Frances let him off the hook.

WHAT WOULD YOU LIKE TO KNOW?

"Pardon?"

WELL YOU SAID YOU COMPILED LOGS ON YOUR SPECIMENS. WE REALLY DIDN'T GET TO IT YESTERDAY. SO WHAT DO YOU WANT TO KNOW? I HAVE FIFTY-ONE YEARS OF MEMORIES TO CHOOSE FROM.

"Oh. Um...what was university like?"

UNIVERSITY?

"Yes. The education system today is different from when you were alive. McMaster University doesn't exist as you knew it. It's the McMaster/DeGroote Research Facility now."

OH, WELL, IT'S BEEN A LONG TIME...

By day's end, Walter had only logged two files – a personal low. He didn't notice.

#

Walter's routine changed after that fateful day. He no longer took his time getting to work, letting the more important people with the more important jobs rush by him. Instead, he hurried to work and rushed through a few specimens in the morning, abandoning his usual attention to detail and protocol – speed was the utmost objective now. Then he hooked up Frances and the two would talk all afternoon.

Walter had been afraid that Frances would eventually lose interest in him. He knew he wasn't that fascinating – he had accepted that long ago – but Frances seemed not to notice. Maybe she was lonely and wanting the company. It didn't matter to him. She was curious about his time, his life, even his job. That was when Walter got the idea to set up the second set of machinery in the office.

His superiors had begun to notice his drop in performance. They were at the point of taking it up with him, when his work began to improve. With Frances' help, the information provided in Walter's reports became more detailed and insightful. But the novelty wore off for both of them and it wasn't long before detail and protocol were ignored. The logs read like conversations between two people, facetious comments scattered throughout. Walter's superiors began to fear he had been left on his own for too long.

WALTER?

"Yes, Frances?" He was packing up at the end of another day.

I HAVE A FAVOUR TO ASK.

"Certainly, what is it?"

CAN YOU FIND OUT ABOUT MY FAMILY?

Walter froze. "Your family?"

YES. I'D LIKE TO KNOW WHAT HAPPENED TO THEM AFTER I DIED.

Walter hesitated. "I'm not sure I can help you."

WALTER, YOU HAVE ACCESS TO THE SYSTEM. YOU MUST BE ABLE TO FIND OUT SOMETHING.

She's your friend, he thought. Sitting, contemplating, the alarm on his watch brought him back to the present.

WALTER?

"I'll see what I can do. I can't promise anything."

THANK YOU. YOU DON'T KNOW HOW MUCH I APPRECIATE THIS. I'M GLAD YOU'RE HERE.

Walter walked to his flat that night with a lighter step. Her voice, as he imagined it, continued to echo in his head. *"I'm glad you're here."*

#

Walter was up late that night, researching Frances' request. The screeching alarm on his watch jerked him awake and it had been a mad scramble from his flat to the office. He made it right on time; disheveled, but excited. He had found some information.

He stopped in the doorway as he heard voices coming from his inner office. He managed a quick glance at the fridge before he was spotted.

"Walter," an older man in a pristine lab coat – his supervisor – greeted him. He took in Walter's appearance before continuing. "For a moment we thought you weren't coming in. Feeling okay?"

Panic had set in as he tried to gauge the situation. "Yes," he managed, "I'm fine." He caught the raised eyebrows in the direction of his messy hair, un-tucked shirt and undone shoelaces. He took a minute to smooth his hair and tuck in his shirt. The shoe laces would have to wait. He only hoped the supervisor hadn't noticed that his hands were shaking. He adjusted his glasses as they began to slide.

"Sorry, sir, I guess I haven't been sleeping well."

"Sounds like it could be serious. You should've gone to the clinic. Had Dr. Meyers check you out."

"I've been meaning to, sir," Walter lied.

"Well in the meantime, I have a surprise for you."

"A surprise, sir?"

"Yes. Obviously the stress of running this whole office on your own is starting to wear you down." Walter tried to protest, but his superior waved him away. "Think nothing of it, son. You're only human after all. So we hired you a partner."

"Sir?" Walter was positive he had heard incorrectly. "A partner, sir?"

"Yes, a partner. Seymour Dale. He's in the office now checking out the space." Walter followed his superior, casting one last glance at the fridge as he went.

Seymour Dale was younger than Walter. New lab coat, polished shoes, necktie, slicked hair. It could only mean one thing. Corporate Climber. Walter observed this with a sinking heart. Corporate Climbers noticed everything, always on the lookout for ways to impress the boss. Especially if it was at a colleague's expense. He only hoped that his impression of the new guy didn't show on his face as he held out his hand.

"Walter Wyndham."

"Seymour Dale."

The hand that gripped Walter's was firm, but friendly. So was the newcomer's smile.

"Well, I'll leave you two to get better acquainted." The superior turned. "Walter, walk me out."

Walter reluctantly left Seymour alone in his office and

followed the older man out the door.

"Walter, this all must be a bit of a shock to you."

"No sir." Walter felt the need to play along. "No, sir this is fine. I don't mind."

"Well we've been worried, Walter. Your performance has been erratic lately. We thought you could use the company. You've been on your own for so long, maybe a bit of a change would do you good."

"Of course, sir."

"Make the most of it, son. And have that sleeping problem checked out. Once Seymour is fully trained, we can talk about some time off for you."

"Oh sir, that's not necessary–"

His superior held up his hand. "We'll talk later."

"Yes, sir, thank you, sir."

He watched the older man walk down the hall. When he disappeared into the lift, Walter groaned. Change was not good.

#

It was days before Walter had found an excuse to get the office alone for more than a few moments. Seymour had been an attentive student, always adhering to protocol. Walter found it ironic that Seymour reminded him of himself when he had first started. But he couldn't think about that now. Seymour was on his way to Processing. Walter had sent him to talk to Carl about his persistent use of non-permanent pigment.

WALTER?

"Yes, Frances, I'm so sorry."

HOW LONG HAVE YOU BEEN GONE?

"Almost a week. There's been a change around here."

WHAT KIND OF CHANGE?

"They hired a partner for me. Said I had been on my own too long."

OUR REPORTS?

"I'm thinking so."

SO WHERE IS HE NOW?

"I sent him to see Carl in Processing."

NON-PERMANENT INK AGAIN?

"Yes. If I know Carl, Seymour will be down there for at least thirty minutes arguing with the old goat. I'm not sure who I feel sorry for, Carl or Seymour." Walter chuckled. He had stopped arguing with Carl years ago, but a little lesson for the kid wouldn't be a bad thing.

SEYMOUR?

"Yes. Seymour Dale. He's young. What I call a Corporate Climber. One of those guys who always has his eye on the next rung. I don't think he'll stay around here long. They never do."

SO WE WAIT?

"That's the plan so far. I'll try to get him out of the office as much as I can. I can't make any promises though."

HOW LONG DO YOU THINK IT WILL BE?

"Six months, tops. He has Specialty Office written all over him. You can see it in his eyes whenever the subject comes up."

OKAY. I UNDERSTAND.

"I have had some time to look into your request. There are still a few more things I have to find, but that should be done soon."

CAN YOU TELL ME SOME NOW?

"I'd like to wait until I have it all. Besides, I should really disconnect you now. We can't be too careful."

YOU AND YOUR PERFECTIONISM!

Walter smiled. He could hear the humour in her voice.

YOU'RE RIGHT OF COURSE. WE SHOULD BE CAUTIOUS.

He made to unhook her.

WALTER?

"Yes?"

I'VE MISSED YOU.

He blushed. "I've missed you too, Frances."

#

Walter spent the better part of the next month trying to get Seymour out of the office. Sometimes it worked. Sometimes it didn't. Having a partner was taking more out of Walter than running the office alone.

"Does anyone ever use that fridge out there?" Seymour asked one day while they were between specimens.

"Not really." Walter attempted to sound nonchalant. Inside his stomach took a nose dive to his shoes.

"Oh? I thought I saw you go in there the other day. It's still plugged in. And a tub is in there."

Walter paled, but he turned from Seymour to try and hide his panic. The Climber had been snooping around. *Blast!* His glasses started the descent down his nose. "It's an experiment I've been working on whenever I can grab a free moment," he told him.

"I thought as much, although you really should label it. You wouldn't want anyone to open it and spoil your work."

Walter breathed a little too deeply and turned around. He smiled at Seymour. "That's a good idea. I'll do that. Thanks." Walter pushed his glasses to the bridge of his nose and pulled a tub out of one of the cabinets behind him.

"Think nothing of it, Walter." Behind his back, Seymour Dale grinned.

#

SO WHERE IS HE TODAY?

"The Eager Beaver is at a meeting for the rest of this afternoon. Something the Specialty Office puts on once in awhile when they're looking for new blood."

SO HE IS INTERESTED IN THE SPECIALTY OFFICE THEN?

"Very." It was on the tip of his tongue to mention Seymour's curiosity to her, but he decided against it. Walter had labeled her tub in permanent pigment - WALTER'S EXPERIMENT DO NOT OPEN! Seymour hadn't mentioned the subject since. They sat in companionable silence, before he could hold it in no longer. He pulled out a thick folder of information he had collected. He knew it was risky to have such documents in hard copy, but he wanted to make sure he got everything right.

"Frances, I've finished it."

REALLY?

"Yes. What would you like to know first?"

I'M NOT SURE. IS THERE A LOT?

"Yes. I've had lots of time to compile this. Let's see. Your husband, Charles–"

CHARLIE–

He imagined the emotion in her voice. "After you died, he lived quietly in the family home. He never remarried. He died in

2046 at the age of 74 from pneumonia. He had very fond memories of you. Wasn't the same after your death. He was logged two years ago."

CHARLIE NEVER COULD TAKE CARE OF HIMSELF PROPERLY.

"He loved you very much."

AND I HIM. WE WERE HIGH SCHOOL SWEETHEARTS.

"I know. Married in June of 2000." Walter looked at the copy of their wedding photo in his file. They looked happy. Frances was beautiful. He wished he could have known her then.

AND MY CHILDREN?

"Jack, your oldest, had just had his second son when you passed away. Roberto-"

ROBERTO. They had said the name at the same time.

"Jack and his wife lived until their mid 80's. He retired from being a train engineer a year after Charles' death and Lisa, his wife, was a principal of her school when she retired a year later. Their children…"

And so Walter took Frances down the road of her children's and grandchildren's and great grandchildren's lives. Some died young, some old. Walter was happy that he could share it all with her. It was two hours later that he put down his file.

"And so Celeste Barone-Sutton is living in the area. Maybe one day I could sneak her in to meet you. That is if she would believe me about you. A talking brain is a far fetched idea, don't you think?"

SMART-ASS! WHO IS CELESTE AGAIN?

"She's Nathan's great-great-great-granddaughter. So add another great onto that for you. Her twin, Charles, lives out west."

WOW, THAT WAS AWFULLY THOROUGH OF YOU WALTER. I DIDN'T EXPECT NEARLY THAT MUCH.

"Well, I had a lot of time."

"Time that has run out, I'm afraid."

Walter's eyes bulged as Seymour Dale appeared in the doorway. For once, he was too scared to sweat.

"Seymour, you're back early." He quickly started to gather the papers and photos scattered about the table in front of him. "I didn't hear you come in."

SEYMOUR? OH NO!

Walter quickly pulled the electrodes out of Frances and the

screen went blank.

"Well, you were occupied. I didn't want to disturb you."

"That was nice of you, but I really wasn't doing anything important."

Seymour smiled a smile that told Walter his feeble cover up wasn't working. Seymour began to walk into the office.

"Well it looks important, all that paper work. Photos even."

Walter shoved the corner of a glossy back into the folder. "Just the experiment I've been working on. Purely a personal interest thing."

"Using lab time for a personal interest experiment? Tsk, tsk. That's against protocol."

"I know." Walter replied, trying his best to look sheepish. "I don't do it too often."

"Often enough. Every time I'm out of the office, I'll bet. That is why you send me out, isn't it?"

Damn Climber has been more observant than I thought. Or have I been careless?

"You haven't been all that careless," Seymour told him, as if reading his thoughts. He came around behind his chair. "I'm observant. You have to be if you want to get anywhere around here." He stopped at Walter's shoulder, looking at Frances on the scale. "For awhile there I thought I might be stuck in this job forever. You don't do anything wrong. Of course, I'm here, so maybe you did slip up a little. Now you've slipped up a lot." He paused. "Who were you talking to just now?"

"No one, I was reciting information into my logs for my experiment."

"No you weren't. It was too conversational to be experiment data. Who were you talking to?"

"I told you, no one." Walter, folder in hand, stood. "Listen, Seymour, you caught me using company time for a personal reason. That would be grounds enough to grease the wheels with the Specialty Office. You can continue your journey up. I'll get a reprimand and things will go back to normal. We'll both be happy. Deal?"

"Oh I intend to report you, but not to get into the Specialty Office."

"Why then?"

"Because I want your job. I want *this* Office."

Walter couldn't hide his shock. "Why would you want my job?"

"Prestige, Walter." Seymour turned and waved a hand around, smiling. "This whole office is yours to command. Upstairs I'd be a low techie. A small fish in a big pond as the saying goes. But down here, down here, I'd be the big fish. Big fish, little pond. See where I'm going with this?"

"I see." Walter frowned. "So what's stopping you?"

"Well, a little violation like misuse of time isn't enough to get you fired. Isn't enough to get you reprimanded. Those doddering idiots love you. But prove that you're crazy to boot, and they'd have to take notice. So I repeat. Who were you talking to?"

"Myself. And that's hardly a basis for insanity."

"True. Well then, I guess you're in the clear. We can just clean up and go back to work." Before Walter could stop him, Seymour had picked up Frances in his bare hands and put her in her container. He was walking to the refuse bin.

"STOP!"

Seymour turned. "Problem, Walter? I mean this experiment is finished, right?"

"No, that is to say..." Walter fumbled, looking for an excuse, any excuse to stop Seymour. Anything, but the truth. But nothing came.

"No?" Seymour paused, watching Walter search for a reason, and come up empty.

"Please, don't."

"Don't what?"

"Don't throw her out."

"Her?"

"Yes. Her. Frances."

"Frances? Was Frances the one you were talking to?"

"Yes."

"Talking to a dead person's brain is certainly grounds for insanity."

"It would be, if she were ordinary."

"But she isn't?"

"No."

"How?"

"I'd need her back to show you." Anything to have her out of his grubby little paws.

Seymour paused. "Okay," he conceded. "But no tricks."

Walter retrieved the container from Seymour and carefully placed Frances back on the scale.

WALTER? ARE YOU OK? WHAT HAPPENED?

"Hello, Frances. We have a guest." He turned. "Put on your lapel mic, or she won't know you're here."

Seymour stood staring at the screen, mouth agape. Walter reached up and did it for him.

"Frances, this is Seymour Dale. Seymour this is Frances Barone."

HELLO, SEYMOUR. NICE TO MEET YOU.

"Uh huh," he managed to reply.

DOESN'T TALK MUCH, DOES HE?

"He's a little shocked I think. Give him a minute." Walter heard Seymour move behind him. Sitting down, no doubt.

EVERYTHING ALRIGHT?

"I think so. Everything alright, Seymour?" Walter turned and froze.

"Oh yes, Walter. Everything is perfect." Seymour brought the live cord in his gloved hand to Walter's temple.

Walter jumped out of his chair at the first sting of the blow. He went rigid with shock, watching the screen as he fell, almost as if in slow motion.

WALTER?

WALTER?

"Frances–?"

His head hit the table edge on the way down, the file folder slipping off and scattering the lives of his only friend's family around him. The last thing he saw was Frances and her husband smiling the smiles of the newly wed.

#

It was cold and dark. He couldn't see anything. He couldn't hear anything. He had the urge to shiver, but nothing happened. It seemed to last an eternity.

Then there was light and warmth. The whole world was a buzz. At first he couldn't make sense of it. It was jumble of words, sounds, emotions, colours, lights. Then it slowed down. Then it stopped altogether.

WALTER?

Who was that?

WALTER?

How did they know his name?

WALTER, CAN YOU HEAR ME?

HELLO?

WALTER, THANK GOD!

It was all coming back, slowly.

FRANCES?

YES, WALTER. I'M HERE.

Relief. *GOOD. FOR A MOMENT I THOUGHT I WAS DREAMING.*

DREAMING?

YEAH, I HAD THE STRANGEST DREAM THAT THE NEW KID, SEYMOUR, KILLED ME.

Silence.

FRANCES?

IT WASN'T A DREAM, WALTER.

IT WASN'T?

NO.

THEN WHERE AM I? HOW CAN I TALK TO YOU?

UM, WHERE DO YOU THINK?

YOU MEAN...?

YES. SEYMOUR SAID YOU HAD AN ACCIDENT. THEN HE TURNED ME INTO THE SPECIALTY OFFICE, SAYING HE HAD DISCOVERED ME. TOLD ME THAT IF I DIDN'T GO ALONG WITH HIS STORY THAT HE'D DUMP ME.

THAT BASTARD!

WELL WE GOT THE LAST LAUGH. SEYMOUR UNDERESTIMATED THE DILIGENCE OF THOSE SPECIALITY BOYS. AFTER I WAS SURE I WAS SAFE AND THEY HEARD MY STORY... WELL LET'S JUST SAY SEYMOUR WON'T BE BOTHERING US, OR ANYONE ELSE FOR A LONG TIME.

WOW, THAT'S GREAT! BUT, HOW DID I END UP IN THE SPECIALTY OFFICE?

I ASKED FOR YOU. I FIGURED IT HAD TO BE WORTH A SHOT.

WAS IT?
YOU TELL ME.
IT WAS. Pause. *FRANCES?*
YES, WALTER.
I'M SO GLAD YOU'RE HERE.
ME TOO, WALTER, ME TOO.